D1053718

A FRIEND
FROM ENGLAND

BY THE SAME AUTHOR

The Debut
Providence
Look at Me
Hotle du Lac
Family and Friends
The Misalliance

A FRIEND FROM ENGLAND

PANTHEON

BOOKS

NEW YORK

ANITA BROOKNER

First American Edition
Copyright © 1987 by Selobrook Ltd.

All rights reserved under International and Pan-American Copyright
Conventions. Published in the United States by Pantheon Books, a
division of Random House, Inc., New York, and simultaneously in
Canada by Random House of Canada Limited, Toronto.
Originally published in Great Britain
by Jonathan Cape Ltd., London

Library of Congress Cataloging-in-Publication Data
Brookner, Anita.
A friend from England.
I. Title.
PR6052.R5816F7   1987   823'.914   87-46049
ISBN 0-394-56387-5

Manufactured in the United States of America

FOR CARMEN CALLIL

A FRIEND FROM ENGLAND

O N E

I FIRST got to know Oscar Livingstone in fairly humdrum circumstances. He was an accountant, in a small way of business, with a few faithful and unambitious clients. I had inherited him from my father, who had also been in a small way of business, and I would go to his tiny office in Southampton Row once a year for a routine inspection of my bills and receipts; he would offer no advice about exciting ways of diversifying or investing, and I found this extremely restful, the whole transaction taking on something of the enactment of a religious office, in which both Oscar and I knew our responses and after which we shook hands gravely, and then relaxed into an exchange of equally ritualistic questions about our respective families. My own family was largely in the past, but Oscar was married to a woman who looked so remarkably like him that I had always assumed her to be his sister on those occasions when she came in to do a bit of typing for him. They were a placid, wistful couple, and when my visits coincided with their both being in the office they would gaze at me with large sympathetic eyes and commiserate with me all over again on small and large losses, both financial and familial, which I in my absent-mindedness had consigned for contemplation to the odd empty afternoon, or perhaps the late evening, or, more properly, had forgotten about altogether.

So established was this ritual that the news of Oscar's astonishing piece of luck was all the more surprising, although it did not disturb his expression, except for adding a furrow to his previously untroubled brow. His wife, Dorrie, had come into the office to help him bear the burden of his good fortune, and she gazed at me with an almost tragic fixity as she imparted the news. 'We wanted you to hear directly,' she said, 'before the rumours started flying. Although we did say we wanted no publicity.' It appeared that Oscar had had an extremely substantial win on the football pools. They could not bring themselves to name the sum, but they assured me that they would no longer have to worry about the future, and then, as if to put my mind at rest, told me that although Oscar would be giving up his office, he would continue to see to my tax returns if I would take them to him at his house in Wimbledon. 'Oh, no, we shan't be moving,' said Dorrie. 'Just a few little additions to the home. And something for our daughter, of course.'

When the time came round for my annual financial consultation, I found it entirely natural to speak to Oscar again, and the same queries were offered and answered, although he was now a millionaire (rumour had, of course, escalated the sum into two or even five millions) and I, like my father, was now in a small way of business. The only difference was that when I telephoned to ask if I might make an appointment to see him at his house, his voice seemed to have taken on a nostalgia and also a sleepiness which I put down to the fact of his retirement and the indolence bred in him from merely having to move from one room to another instead of stepping out each morning and encountering the challenge of a difficult journey on tubes and buses. It occurred to me to wonder how he had faced the prospect of working in central London, distant as it was from his suburban home, for so many years. As far as I could see, he was so unassuming as to appear endangered: he brought his lunch in a selection of bags in his briefcase, and did not trust the sort of food that everybody else ate or was obliged to eat. Or perhaps Dorrie did not trust it for him. Once, when I had had an early afternoon appointment, I had found him delicately peeling an orange into an empty box file, evidently designated for that purpose, and on another occasion I noticed a complicated bouquet of Brie and something pungent and sweet. 'What did you have for lunch?' I asked him, eager to penetrate this mystery. He answered the question with the same gravity as that with which he responded to my enquiries about Value Added Tax. 'Dorrie put me up some biscuits and cheese,' he said. 'And a slice of the pineapple we had last night for dinner.' He had always impressed me as home-loving and uxorious, mildly inert, a bulky soft-voiced man with beautifully cared-for hands, something about him broadcasting the resignation of a schoolboy who has to submit to an inspection before he is allowed to leave the house.

He had always seemed pleased to see me, which was flattering, for I was nothing like my father, who had been something of a friend to him, and when I telephoned he warned me that Dorrie was about to issue an invitation to dinner. It was natural to him to assume that our association would continue over and above the call of the Inland Revenue, and I was touched that he should remember me when this sudden influx of money might seem to promise them a different life. But Oscar was a very steadfast man and indeed spread about him an aura of benign pessimism which somehow went with his profession. I liked to think of him relaxing in Wimbledon with Dorrie, and I found myself quite looking forward to seeing them both again, and to talking over this astonishing turn of fortune. I had never known anyone so scandalously rich before, and I wanted to see if it had changed them. I imagined that the possession of wealth made itself known through some kind of stigmata: I foresaw difficulties in getting through the eye of a needle, and wondered if the strain would show. Above all, I wanted to see their house and with it

11

Dorrie's improvements. Living austerely myself, I enjoyed luxury in others.

I was not disappointed. The house – a substantial but essentially modest suburban villa – was furnished with voluptuous grandeur in approximations of various styles, predominantly those of several Louis, with late nineteenth- and early twentieth-century additions. Heavy coloured glass ashtrays of monstrous size and weight rested on inlaid marquetry tables of vaguely Pompadour associations. At dinner we drank champagne from ruby Bohemian glasses: the meat was carved at a Boulle-type sideboard. 'Regency' wallpaper of dark green and lighter green stripes was partially covered by gilt-framed landscapes of no style whatever. The dining-room seemed dark, as dining-rooms often do. In fact all the rooms seemed to repel both light and weather; they were designed to keep one's thoughts indoors, resigned and melancholy. I thought of listless Saturday afternoons, when I pictured Oscar relaxing in one of the turquoise silk-covered bergères, with footstools to match. I thought of Dorrie taking a nap in her shell-pink bedroom with the extravagant expanses of white shag-pile carpet. All the windows would be closed, of course, the smell of a substantial lunch still heavy on the air, slightly obscured by one of the two or three weekend cigars. Upstairs, the nap finished, and the light already beginning to fade, I imagined Dorrie switching on the vaguely baronial gas fire and pulling the satin curtains. Throwing a handful of flowery cologne over her throat and shoulders, she would change into a patterned silk dress, taking a clean handkerchief and tucking it up her sleeve. It would not be quite time for tea, but as relatives were expected she would start her preparations in the kitchen, transferring home-made cakes and biscuits on to dishes with gold rims, and laying cups and plates, interleaved with tiny napkins of écru linen, on the trolley, knives and spoons tinkling, to be wheeled in effortlessly at the right moment. For she was daintily houseproud.

I found it all very cosy. Although their life seemed to depress Oscar and his wife, both of whom had a vaguely disappointed air, I could see myself transformed into just such a virtuous member of just such a successful but melancholy family. I could see myself running baths in my pale pink bathroom and scenting them with expensive essences; I could see myself switching on the television next to my courtesan's bed; I could see myself making quantities of food for the freezer, or, on a sunny day, sitting cautiously out on the terrace, a cut-glass pitcher of orange juice next to me on the dazzlingly painted white wooden table. Days would pass without reference to the outside world. No letters would come through the post, for kinship would be maintained by means of the telephone. I appreciated the ferocious central heating and even the sadness that seemed to go with all these acquisitions, as if the middle years signified just such comfort and just such disenchantment. Youthful impulse or folly, of which not a trace remained, had retreated to the images in those silver photograph frames that crowned the bookcase and the downstairs television: in them, younger versions of Oscar and Dorrie appeared hesitant, in uncharacteristic sunshine, as if awaiting their mature bulk and their natural setting, indoors.

For their present life was the apotheosis of everything that pertained to indoors, and the seasons would revolve without their being much disturbed. Late nights would be theirs, and many snacks: three-course teas and five-course dinners, their large family supplying most of the appetite and all the conversation. When all the sisters and the brothers-in-law were assembled, as they were on the first occasion that I was invited to tea, it took some courage to enter their discourse, which consisted of references beyond or to the side of one, yet they were

13

kindly people, and after one visit, which I thought a total failure, they apparently referred to the occasion amongst themselves or related it to a sister, a brother-in-law, as if it had been important or at least interesting. This touched me, for I was susceptible to their modesty, their rituals, all of which seemed to spell a certain timidity with regard to the outside world, a world from which Oscar had been miraculously freed by the intervention of chance. I responded to their invitations, which were repeated, as if having come once I was bound to be included again, possibly for ever; I sat on one of the many-styled sofas, obediently eating the tiny sandwiches, the little filled rolls, and the various cakes, listening to their calm uninflected voices, and studying what seemed to me to be the superior style of their daughter, Heather. Heather's visit was the ostensible pretext for the monumental tea that was always on offer: it was understood that Heather would never come home to dinner, having more exciting and mysterious plans for the evening. These she would not explain, but would murmur vaguely about going round to someone's house, and it was assumed that all her friends were as well off and as dull of mind as Heather herself. Actually, I believe she was extremely shrewd, but she somehow impressed one as having no inappropriate desires or ambitions. Her parents had looked after her so well, and provided for her so amply, that she had no need to emulate a life other than the one she was already leading, and I knew that Oscar and Dorrie had already set her up in a comfortable service flat in Portman Square. From what I managed to glimpse, on my one brief visit to this flat, it contained the same lush hybrid furnishings as the house in Wimbledon.

Like her mother, Heather had a generous and at the same time melancholy attitude to her wealth and possessions. She would insist on driving me home, in her immaculate new car, as if she had nothing better to do,

14

and as if the fabled evening could wait. She was in no hurry, and something told me that she would have been just as happy at home as she was in Portman Square, pretending to be in the fashion business, but actually managing the boutique which Oscar had bought for her after his windfall. Despite her scornful and up-to-date appearance – the schoolboy's hairstyle, the flat shoes, the long skirt, and the dangling earrings – she was a passive person and would have been content to shelter under the protection of her parents, going with them to their entertainments, accompanying them on their holidays, and eventually marrying a man who had been mediated through the various filters that separated the Livingstones from the rest of humanity. Instead, she did what was expected of her, appeared to enjoy what her parents had provided for her, and enacted for their benefit the emancipated image that they, greatly daring and humble, had imagined that she desired. In this way she repaid them, although I never heard her utter more than monosyllables in their presence. It was, I suppose, honourable of her to accommodate the wilder fling of their imagination in this way. As I say, Heather was shrewd.

It soon became clear to me that Oscar and Dorrie thought me a suitable companion for Heather, and that the strain of melancholy I had detected in that house had something to do with Heather's destiny, which had not yet declared itself. Far from being a problem to them, Heather was docile; rather than the expected rebellion, she had presented them with a temperament as undemanding as that of a Victorian matron, and I say matron rather than virgin because Heather's manner always struck me as extremely grown-up, whereas her expectations of the world were, like those of her parents, somewhat fearful. She was always very nice to her aunts and uncles, interested in their activities, which I found indistinguishable, willing to compare accounts of shopping triumphs or disappointments, rather as if she were the same age as they were. She had a mature attitude, too, to ills of the flesh, professing to know all about ailments and remedies, although she was in the prime of life and not yet a martyr to anything, let alone the rheumatisms, the sinusitis, and the incipient ulcers that had cast their shadow over the brothers-in-law: she always knew someone who suffered in the same way, and was thus able to offer the names of specialists or chiropractors. She was, for instance, able to say of her assistant's mother that she had been to 'all the best men' but had obtained instant relief from acupuncture. She was extraordinarily earnest as she discussed this, giving a foretaste of the woman she would become. In fact the woman she would become was not much different from the girl she already was, and there seemed no reason to suppose that she would ever change or develop or move away from the family circle. Whereas most parents would view this with something like relief, Oscar and Dorrie would sigh inwardly and contemplate their daughter with a mild bewilderment that contained a minute quantum of despair.

Heather's pale milk-fed appearance, effortlessly triumphing over her modish black garments, differed not a lot from that of her mother, or indeed that of her father, and the same air of placid resignation seemed to emanate from all three of them. Their attitude to their good fortune was one of submission, and they seemed to be spending their money more in the line of duty than of pleasure. Occasionally I would see something in Dorrie's face that reminded me of the wistful, complicated attitudes of my own mother, although the two women had never met, while Oscar sometimes looked as if he were contemplating a harsher future than the one that had been assigned to him. Although they had no reason to be unhappy, they were not altogether happy, and they were too innocent to recognize their condition as pertaining to age rather than to substance. The time of reckoning was upon them: if they had ever wished for anything, they now realized that life had moved them on from logical fulfilment of those wishes. They were settled, they were more than comfortable, and likely to remain so, for Oscar had invested their money very wisely. And yet they were not as satisfied as they had expected to be. I am sure that Oscar sometimes regretted his little office and his box files and his onerous journeys on public transport; although he would have been happier working, he would have felt ashamed to carry on as before, thinking it somehow in keeping to be superannuated now that fate had removed him from the category of those who need to be seen to earn their money. Dorrie had probably changed less: her life was not much different from how it had been in earlier days, a reverent addiction to fine housekeeping. Yet they seemed to depend on each other more now that they were always together than they had when long periods of time had kept them apart. 'Where are you going, dear?' one would say to the other as a move was made towards the door of whatever room they were sitting in. And, 'Where's your mother?' Oscar would say to Heather, if Dorrie happened to be absent for more than a minute. The end of their respective siestas would be marked by deep sighs, as if, once reclaimed by the business of ordinary life, they could say goodbye to free will.

The atmosphere in their house was marked by a perpetual Sabbath calm, yet as I only ever visited at weekends I suppose this was entirely appropriate. I had occasion to visit them rather frequently because I had recently come into a small legacy that was hedged around with obscure legal problems, something to do with imprecise wording in the will, on which Oscar seized with an element of his old professionalism. Actually, I believe a solicitor could have cleared the matter up without much difficulty, but I sensed that Oscar welcomed the opportunity to investigate, to make telephone calls in the small garden room designated as his office, and to treat me once more as a ward who needed his advice. At one period I went there nearly every weekend, and once my business was settled the habit was formed: it was even decreed that Heather could pick me up in her car and bring me to Wimbledon as well as taking me home afterwards, rather as if I were a small child going out to tea with her friend's parents. Probably they thus hoped to seal the alliance between Heather and myself, although we had nothing in common beyond an attachment to Oscar and Dorrie. Heather was apparently more mature than I was, but I had reason to doubt the reality of this apparent maturity; in any event, Dorrie seemed to think that I was the more sensible of the two, which was not the case. She would summon me into the kitchen, on the pretext of wrapping up cakes for both of us to take home, and ask, 'How do you think she's looking?', while in the drawing-room Heather would be discoursing on some form of illness with every appearance of adult commitment. We would all sit down and drink a glass of sherry before Heather and I left: although their sherry was of the highest quality, and the glasses fragile and of a pleasing shape, this ritual was accompanied by an involuntary wince on the part of Oscar and Dorrie. They hated anything sour or sharp, but they confessed to liking the smell of the sherry, which somehow added itself to the vanilla of the cakes and the cigar smoke and the closed-in warmth and Dorrie's flowery scent. It felt sophisticated to them, and although their standard of comfort was very high they went on adding to it conscientiously, in the same way as they habitually added to Heather's birthright, so that the car, on our return journey, would be packed with parcels, the fruits of a week's shopping on Dorrie's part, for although she

18

looked as if she never left the house, she now recognized the more exclusive department stores as her natural habitat and embarked on a shopping expedition once or twice a week, no doubt with the same expression of resignation that she wore at home.

Once admitted to the family circle, I found myself falling into the same docility as that which characterized Oscar and Dorrie and Heather: it was pleasing to me to be thus returned to childhood, although I was quite aware that Dorrie looked to me, as a true adult, to induct Heather into the finer mysteries of life. I suppose she thought I might make her a little less amiably incurious, that I might be the cause of her ascending to a self-awareness that would protect her from the wickedness of the world, for they knew that she was still too much their child, and moreover a child with a great deal of money in the background. It was not that they feared fortune hunters, for they longed for her to be married, much as they longed for her to be grown-up, as if only in realizing this condition would she free them from the anxiety they both felt in her presence. They did not fear fortune hunters – indeed, they would have welcomed one, if he were amiable enough – but they had a true sense of the dangers that threaten the unwary. When they saw Heather chatting to her aunts, her brutal haircut crowning her innocent face, her feet in their goblin shoes planted, like those of a schoolgirl, on the lavishly flowered carpet, their mouths pursed, and their eyes seemed to be looking inwards. Their good daughter, who came home to them every weekend, and telephoned every day, was the world to them, or rather that part of the world that they could spare from contemplation of each other, and yet they wished her otherwise, still theirs, but someone else's as well, someone whose supervision would replace their own, leaving them in that state of latency which they, in their timorous dealings with the world, found to be their true climate.

19

It was for this reason, as well as the affection which they naturally and unassumingly felt for young people, that they welcomed my presence. They felt that I had been emancipated by the loss of my own parents, that this had made me stronger, more self-reliant. How I was to impart all this to Heather was quite unclear to me, since she seemed to treat me rather as Dorrie treated her, and would display the same sort of concern for my comfort as Dorrie did for everyone in her house. She would tuck a rug over my legs in the car, partly out of hospitality and partly out of affection for the rug, which her mother had bought for her quite recently and which had been one of the weekend presents. Although I never attempted to get on intimate terms with her, for I found the effort of asking leading questions somehow too onerous to be undertaken, I could feel the force of her passive temperament, and I say temperament rather than personality, for there was little personality in evidence. Perhaps that was what disappointed Dorrie: she came from a generation in which girls were renowned for their personality, and although she gave no sign of it herself she firmly believed in that kind of sprightliness that she mistakenly thought made girls popular. Heather did not smile much, but I put this down to a mild form of distraction: she might, for all I knew, have had an intense inner life, but the impression she gave me was one of opacity. I thought her admirably equipped to deal with her new wealth, for Heather was above all at home with materiality. She had a care for her belongings, for her accessories, her accoutrements, that impressed me as serious; even the way in which she handled the car, in a pair of fine leather gloves assumed for the purpose, was careful, as was the way in which she offered me her own forms of hospitality during the brief moments between my ringing of her doorbell and our leaving for Wimbledon. 'Time for a coffee?' she would say. 'Tea? Drink? No? Shan't be a minute. You'll find some magazines on the table. Help yourself to cigarettes.'

I could quite see why I was supposed to be Heather's passport to the world. Rather older than her, I certainly looked more worldly, particularly to one of Heather's simplicity. There was something disarming about her, and this had to do not so much with lack of intelligence, although she did not seem too bright to me, as with that quality of innocence that she had inherited from her parents. I felt that for all her material assurance, her familiarity with the good things of life, Heather would always need to be accompanied in order that no one should take advantage of her. And this was what both Oscar and Dorrie felt as well. It took me a good while to get used to this idea because of the gulfs in communication that stretched between them. Their conversation was largely meaningless, which I found very restful, until the aunts and brothers turned up with news of the outside world. Left to themselves, and this now seemed to include myself, they were largely ruminant. 'Well, dear,' Oscar would say, levering himself out of his too soft chair. 'There you are. Seen your mother?' And to me, 'Well, Rachel. Nice to see you. Sit down, there's a good girl.' And while Heather went off to bring her mother back from wherever she had been going – it was usually to the kitchen – Oscar and I would subside into a state of mild companionship, the day safely concluded, as if our arrival were all that was needed, and no amount of information we might bring was necessary.

I still see Oscar rising from his chair to greet us. He carried his bulk well, and he always wore a dark suit and a very white shirt, although his ties were a little more interesting now than they had been in the days of Southampton Row. He and Dorrie were not the sort of people to dress in elaborate leisure wear when they were at home: indeed, it always seemed to me that they dressed up for our visits. I see Oscar laying aside the

newspaper and smoothing down his tie, waiting politely for us to establish ourselves before enquiring for
Dorrie and requesting us to bring her back. I see now
that he feared for the safety of his daughter because she
was in some way responsible for the peace and prosper-
ity of his wife. And Dorrie thought of Heather as not
only a loved child but as someone who might cause
Oscar to worry. They saw each other exclusively in
personal terms. It always surprised me that they were
less impressed by the way that Heather ran her boutique
than anxious to know what she was doing with her free
time. Was she eating properly? This seemed to me an
odd question to ask of a woman of twenty-seven, but I
supposed that all parents worried about their children's
diet. Mine had not, which was why I found it so
delightful to sit and be fed by Dorrie, whose food was a
magnificent celebration, on an unimaginable scale of
magnitude, of infant tastes. This was why I found it so
delightful, too, to adapt my own anxieties, which were
of a much more complicated order, to those of the
Livingstones, for although I could see that they were
worried I could not take their worries very seriously.
Indeed, I was aware that they gave themselves over to
these worries as a sort of luxury, and I felt their
consciences were perhaps too fine for the real world.
Dorrie's most characteristic remark was, 'I hope I did
the right thing.' This remark would crop up at intervals
later in the afternoon, when the sisters and brothers-in-
law were assembled. These relatives constituted a sort
of moral court of enquiry, to which Dorrie would feel
bound to submit her case. Even if she took a defective
article back to the shop from which she had bought it
the day before, she would feel ashamed. Even if some
act of rudeness had been perpetrated against her, as
when a man had jostled her when they were both after a
taxi in Piccadilly, she would worry. 'I simply said to
him, "You won't mind if I take this, will you? I believe

22

I was first." ' And then, with a crumpled expression, 'I hope I did the right thing.'

The sisters and brothers-in-law I found less interesting because more worldly. Oscar's brother Sam was a solicitor married to a rather silly woman called Ann who had nothing very much to say for herself. Dorrie's sisters, Janet and Rosemary, and their husbands, Gerald and Lawrence, were sharper versions of Dorrie and seemed to regard her with the same mixture of love and anxiety as that which she lavished on Heather. Far from envying her her wealth they were mildly perturbed that this might expose her to some sort of trouble. They seemed disposed to offer a great deal of advice; conversely, Dorrie felt called upon to give an account of her activities, down to the last purchase or the last encounter. The brothers-in-law were amiable, rather supine men, as men tend to be when married to nervous critical women, and their task in life was to calm their wives down. Dorrie tended to become even more self-doubting when in the presence of her sisters, whose misgivings about Heather were rather too apparent. They both boasted married daughters, and obviously felt that the time had come for action to be taken regarding poor Heather. I must say that of them all only Heather was completely unaware of her failing; she really thought that her aunts and uncles turned up only to see Oscar and Dorrie, and I daresay they did, for they were a remarkably close-knit family. But while Heather offered her earnest advice, which, as a member of the emancipated young, she felt it incumbent upon her to do, I could see the sisters occasionally exchanging looks heavy with preoccupation. In these encounters Heather's age seemed to be fluctuating or negotiable: young enough to be patronized yet much too old to be single, old enough to know about female complaints yet too young to have any. I could see that nobody would relax until they were all brought together to discuss the wedding plans. 'And what about Rachel?' Gerald or Lawrence or Janet would say. 'Any steady boy-friends?' For they were at heart so unspoiled as to think that all boy-friends were steady.

I remember them for their very real kindness and for the becalmed state into which they put one. As we sat among the cake-stands, and the sherry was produced, as the sun outside the tightly shut window declined yet sent strong beams after a recent small shower, as the harmless talk was conducted over my head, I reviewed them in an entirely affectionate and favourable light. Even their slight melancholy, present in Oscar's smiling silence, in Dorrie's invitation to stay on 'for a light supper', as if she feared our departure, in the sisters' stern affection and the brothers' eventually turning to each other to discuss the news of the outside world, enchanted me. I felt as if I were in the presence of a distinct culture, rather like the one that had prevailed in the Russian novels I so enjoyed, in which endless days are spent sitting on terraces, and the feckless elder brother worries the nervous married sister and the wan younger daughter is consumed with passion for an unsuitable student, and the retainers enter the drawing-room with the familiarity of long association. I had that same sensation of time being endlessly capacious, and memory and melancholy being equally tyrannical, the sense of strong feeling and deep family commitment, the same insulation from the world, and above all the self-sufficiency. I had no doubt that in her old age Heather would look back on these afternoons with the same sense of loss. What meads, what kvasses were drunk, what pies were baked at Oblomovka! Even I, disaffected and partly disillusioned as I was, could feel myself being overtaken by these padded afternoons, these unreal conversations, these respectable bourgeois customs, and the love and comfort that these people offered one another. Yet my main memory of those times, or rather the image that comes most frequently to mind, is not that of Dorrie saying, 'I hope I did the right thing,' or her sisters admiring each other's shoes, or Gerald or Lawrence waving away the offer of more cake, or Sam being given his glass of whisky; it is not even of Heather, dressed up in her boutique garb and talking enthusiastically, but disappointingly to everyone who was listening, about the order she had had from a minor but fairly well-known actress, but of Oscar, rising slowly from his chair, casting aside his newspaper, smoothing down his tie, his smile of welcome almost putting his sadness to flight, and saying, 'Well, dear. There you are. Seen your mother?' Only, much later, when these things had come to mind rather forcefully, I seemed to hear him saying something else. 'Where's your mother?' And, in a look of real anguish, which I had never actually seen on his face, he would, in my mind at least, repeat this. 'Where's your mother?' I would hear. And again, 'Where's your mother?'

T W O

IN order to live alone successfully it is probably
necessary to have an audience, or else to be so steeped
in self-esteem that one's every action is perceived as
ceremonious. With no one to enquire of me, 'What did
you have for lunch?', the question I found myself asking
nearly everyone with whom I was on friendly terms, I
tended to gravitate towards those families whose
domesticity was so engulfing that all I had to do was
listen and marvel at the plenitude of activities simply
living in their midst seemed to engender. The Livingstones, with their serious acquisitions and their dedi-
cated appetites, would have attracted me on this simple
level had I not already been seduced by their very real
qualities: their modesty, their love for one another, their
exemplary family closeness and interaction, and their
fundamental goodwill, which made it entirely natural
for them to include me in their plans. Their hospitality
was of the Biblical kind: the stranger at the gates, the
fatherless, the widow and the orphan were encompassed
by them as a matter of course. Fundamentally, their
very true melancholy, which had no foundation that I
could see, but which was simply a function of their
reflectiveness, led them to need company of an undemanding sort as a barrier against the rest of the world
with its evils and its snares, for they were not armoured,
as most people their age were supposed to be, but rather
at a loss to account for bad behaviour, broken promises,
disillusion, cruelty, sharp practice, having no capacity
to deal with any of this, the daily fare of those who
perceive life as a jungle and grimly negotiate for themselves a passage through it.

Of course, I tried to repay their hospitality. I bought

tickets for the theatre, the ballet, the opera at the Coliseum. These occasions were to my mind only a limited success: the plays I chose were comedies, through which they sat politely, and only Heather enjoyed the ballet. But Heather was not present at our nicest evening, when we went to *La Bohème*. I saw Oscar and Dorrie holding hands tightly throughout the last act, and both dabbed their eyes when the curtain went down. 'Lovely, dear, just lovely. I don't know how we can thank you,' Dorrie said, tucking her handkerchief into her evening bag. Both were very formally dressed, Oscar in a dark suit with a dazzling shirt and a pale tie, Dorrie in a blue silk dress with a beautiful white cashmere shawl. But even here it was a case of *noblesse oblige*: Oscar insisted on taking us out to an extravagant supper, and Dorrie enjoyed looking around at the women and the clothes they were wearing. They were, of course, no strangers to this kind of entertainment; if anything, they were a little worried at being in my company, as if they might offend me if they failed to enjoy themselves. Their pleasure at having been so moved was mixed with relief at not having to utter false expressions of delight. They were so painfully honest that they would have made a poor job of it, but of course they did not know this. 'I'm not good at compliments,' Oscar said, 'but this has been a real treat. Hasn't it, dear?' Dorrie, her eyes already melting again with reminiscences of Mimi's death, replied, 'Just wait until I tell the girls. And how Heather would have loved it. But of course she's out nearly every evening with her friends. And I expect you are too, Rachel,' she added. This last remark was not given the sharp look and the accent of interrogation that her sisters (the girls) would undoubtedly have supplied. Dorrie was without guile and thought that it was natural for young people to be out. For she saw us as young and therefore entitled to pleasure, and she thought, or chose to think, that the

27

pleasures of young people were innocent.

But we were not young. Heather was twenty-seven and I was thirty-two, and we had been working and independent for years. We were young only in the sense that we were not unduly burdened with responsibilities, were not in poor health, and were not married. We were not even a natural pair, for we had nothing in common except Heather's parents. It never occurred to me to wonder what Heather got up to in Portman Square, but if ever I gave it any thought her life, somehow, failed to convince me. I sensed in her no trace of clandestine excitement or secret alliances, no unsuitable friends or dangerous acquaintances. I saw her treating her friends to the same even-tempered and natural hospitality as her parents meted out in Wimbledon. For some reason I saw her friends as predominantly female; there was something unaltered in Heather's placid expression, and this was what gave her aunts pause. They saw in this undemanding girl a sort of incapacity; but what I saw was absence. Like her parents, she was utterly deficient in the desire to do anything dangerous or proprietary, deficient, too, in bad faith, in curiosity, in speculation. She moved through her life not as a sleep-walker, precisely, for I believe she managed her little shop quite efficiently, but rather as a swimmer in calm and protected waters, powered only by the healthy movements of a beautifully functioning organism. Her very steadiness irritated me, until I was even more irritated by the vivacity of her learned responses when she talked to her aunts, but her steadiness also shamed me, as did her habitual mildness.

There was something inherently immovable, or perhaps non-negotiable, about the three of them, but only in Heather did this quality make one a little uncomfortable, as if something were out of joint. For Oscar and Dorrie one had no fears; one knew that they were good, and if they tended to be immovable in this life, there was no doubt that in some future incarnation they would reap the reward promised in the Bible and run to and fro like sparks among the stubble. But there was something artificial about Heather's demeanour, although she was not aware of this; when I thought about it I had the feeling that she was a potential victim. Not the victim of a violent action, exactly, but of a trick. Once I had come upon her, in the hallway of her parents' house, dreamily standing on one leg, large earrings reflecting a beam of sunlight from the glass above the front door, apparently doing nothing. In fact she was reading a postcard which she had picked up from a piece of furniture imitating a Florentine marriage chest, but she gave the strong impression that nothing was taking place. And when she would help to carry in the tea from the kitchen to the drawing-room her head would be bent and her rather long pale neck would emerge from her black sweater as if she had been prepared for execution. One thought of her not exactly as a woman but as some sort of animal known for its unassuming qualities, a heifer, perhaps. Heifers are also traditionally associated with sacrifice. The difficulty with Heather seemed to be that she lacked the emotional equipment even for sacrifice, though sacrifices were planned for her by those watchful aunts. Little parties were arranged by her married cousins, Sarah and Georgina, at which Heather was exhibited to various young men who were said to be acquaintances of their husbands. I was never invited to these ordeals, of course, since it was feared that I might forget the family conspiracy and strike out on my own, but from what I gathered later Heather had failed to play her part, had smiled politely but in evident bewilderment at the ponderous and slightly obscene badinage destined to put her at her ease, and had left early, casting the whole thing into perspective with the words, 'No, thank you, I came in my own car.' These horrible rituals were then

29

further discussed, and at last I began to feel a genuine sympathy for Heather, although I could see that her impenetrability might prove to be a problem for her mother and father.

But supposing that she were happy with matters as they stood? Supposing too that she possessed that genuine mildness of temperament, that latency to which I have referred, that was not only the quality that she shared with her parents but the quality that she could share with nobody else? Supposing that Heather's shrewdness, which I had somehow never doubted, lay in her perception of this fact? Supposing that she had taken stock of her situation and realized, quite calmly and maturely, that she was unfitted for those watchful occasions, at which others, it appeared, were always to be allowed to lay bets, preferring, as a matter of dignity, the quieter manners of her parents' house, with its rituals and its customs so devoid of malicious intention, so maddening to those of a more contentious disposition? Heather could see, as I could, that her mother was superior to those sisters of hers, and that those sisters disguised their largely unconscious envy as exaggerated concern for Heather's well-being. She could even see that their concern was not devoid of a certain prurience, the prurience that some ageing women feel when excluded from the sexual odysseys of the young. Their view of Heather's obduracy was baffling and uncomfortable even to themselves, for they were essentially harmless women who did not fully understand their own mixed motives. I pitied these harmless women, faced with this evidence of their own baseness, and so anxious to disguise its existence that they increased their ostensible anxiety over Heather's unpartnered existence in order to hide its traces. Heather knew all this, of course; her uninflected smile began to seem more complex to me as I saw it as a weapon with which she guarded her virtue.

30

It was probably over the meaning and substance of the concept of virtue that we all came adrift. For myself, the battle was long lost: such shreds of virtue as I retained served only to make me seek it in others, and, when I found it, to be moved beyond all words, ready to defend what I had already forfeited. In this way, my odd relationship with the Livingstones was of great value to me; they were fixed points of reference in a slipping universe, abiding by rules which everybody else had broken. Heather I was eventually willing to take on as a contemporary embodiment, faint but unmistakable, of those rules. I think she had a feeling that she was somehow endangered, or that she belonged to an endangered species, for she sometimes asked my advice on quite simple matters, as if unwilling to reveal her ignorance to others among her contemporaries. And in due course it began to be apparent to me that Oscar and Dorrie regarded me as a chaperone for Heather, whose incapacities may have contributed to their melancholia but whose very integrity and unalterability they cherished. Even the aunts saw me as having some value, or perhaps function would be a better way of putting it, for I doubt if they liked me. 'I'm sure Rachel meets some interesting people in that bookshop of hers,' they would say. 'I'm sure Heather would love to meet them – she was always a great reader.' For they thought I ruled over a sort of Bohemia, and, greatly daring, were willing to trust me with an enterprise at which they had so surprisingly failed.

The truth was, of course, somewhat different. I owned a third of a small bookshop in Notting Hill and there was nothing Bohemian about it. My partners were a pleasant middle-aged woman called Eileen Somers and mild bookish Robin Burt who did most of the work behind the scenes: I preferred to serve. On one decisive afternoon, Heather actually picked me up there. However, she turned politely away while I was seeing to a customer, as if this transaction should not be witnessed. She was wearing a beautiful brown tweed suit and she looked unusually grown-up and independent; however, she smiled indifferently when I asked her if there was anything she would like to take away with her, and then selected a couple of paperbacks as if to please me. These remained in the back of the car: I saw them there a week later. Thus, uncorrupted by other people's information, Heather remained to all intents and purposes incorruptible.

I was however intrigued by the change of attire. The black avant-garde garments had disappeared: Heather was dressed as comfortably-off young women might be expected to dress. In addition to the chestnut suit she wore a pullover of ivory cashmere with a printed silk scarf knotted and tucked into the neck; she carried a handbag rather than a sort of gamekeeper's pouch and her moccasins were the colour of conkers when they first split the green husk and emerge, glistening, to lie among the fallen leaves. She was, of course, as dreamy as ever, and nothing in her manner signalled that any change had taken place. But there was something in the way she handled the car – reversing rather carelessly, remarking on someone else's bad parking – that bore the stamp of an assurance that had not been there before. Heather had always driven her car as if both she and it were competing for an award for good behaviour. She washed and groomed it conscientiously and nothing was allowed to mar its pale interior. On the road she drove steadily, and never did anything to kindle the emotions of other drivers. But on the day in question I noted that her driving was a little less smooth than usual, while on the back seat lay not only the paperbacks she had reluctantly acquired in my shop but several carrier bags from Harrods and some dry cleaning in a sheet of plastic. 'Don't mind the mess,' she said. 'I didn't have time to go home after lunch.' I thought that she was treating me to a hospitality rather more casual, more incidental, than the kind she usually bestowed: she was offering me a glimpse into a crowded life, rather like those women who value one largely as a reflector, and to whom one has to pay one's dues for being allowed to join them for a minute or two on their brilliant upward progress. I do not mean that Heather was suddenly giving herself airs, or finally coming to the realization that she could do as she liked; she was too decent and too genuinely obscure to behave in so parvenu a manner. But I became aware that her life, in those intervals between the weekends, might be subject to some kind of investment, that Heather might actually have some kind of a context independent of that of her parents. The idea intrigued me but it also cheered me up. I had begun to feel uneasy about the pious hopes Oscar and Dorrie might have had that I would somehow look after Heather, guide her towards a radiant future, that I might in fact inherit Heather from her parents when those parents, in obedience to some inner information, decided they could do no more. I had already received hints of this, subliminally, in the mild but dispassionate gaze that Oscar let fall on his only child, in the distant calm of Dorrie's eyes, as she poured tea or handed cakes, in the smile that was always on her face when her drawing-room was full. It was the smile, above all, that registered with me, the smile of a woman who, doing the best she possibly could herself, would warm into greater pleasure at the sight of the good deeds of others. It was a smile that could droop into disappointment at even the rumour of a duty shirked, a burden unborne, a signal not received.

I said, 'You look lovely, Heather. I like the new style. And I love the colours.' She said, quite seriously, but with a hint of professional expertise, 'Well, black isn't quite right for this time of the year, is it?' She inclined her head to the window as she said this, and looking out

33

on my side I saw the prunus trees in flower and the forsythia and the first daffodils. Everything in this suburb reminded one of the gardens of childhood. Pink petals drifted along damp pavements, and through my window I caught the harsh smell of the earth, sour after a long cold winter. The trees were still leafless and the weather uncertain, but the cloudy drizzle was not accompanied by a darkening sky, and the white light seemed to promise long evenings and a quick flowering. I had always loved suburbs. My own life was spent in the landlocked city streets, which suited me well enough since I had odd fears of death by water. But I looked forward to a time when I would occupy a little house with a garden and have people to tea. I was aware that this was the ambition of a child rather than an adult, and this was rather surprising since, as far as I knew, I behaved in a thoroughly grown-up manner. But obviously some part of me yearned to become suburban again and to hear a garden gate click behind me as I set off on summer evenings to meet my friends.

In the meantime I had the Livingstones. And they had me, for in some odd way I felt nearer to Oscar and Dorrie than I did to Heather, although Heather and I were contemporaries and might be thought to have had much in common. In fact I had originally been tried out as a companion for Heather before it had been acknowledged – wordlessly, of course – that I would be better at looking after her, as a sort of surrogate elder, than as a friend and acquaintance. This suited me well enough, for I felt a genuine love for Heather's parents, while feeling rather little for Heather herself. When I say rather little, I mean that I felt a full complement of boredom, irritation, tolerance, and reluctant affection for her. I thought that in view of my function or destiny that was probably enough. Therefore I was both amused and relieved to see her in her new guise, well turned out, possibly with a secret, yet still scrupulously

34

pursing her lips before answering a question and still lowering her head before deciding on an action.

But in the course of the afternoon it began to seem as if Heather had outstripped me, or at least as if she no longer required my custodial care. Rather unusually, she allowed her mother to wait on her, to serve her with tea while she examined her glossy shoes, rotating her right ankle critically as if to examine them from a more professional stance than she usually accorded herself. She said little, as if waiting to be engaged in a topic that interested her rather than contributing eagerly to whatever plangent exchanges were on offer. Even when the aunts arrived, no, particularly when the aunts arrived and settled in to their comments on the week's news and complaints, she held slightly aloof, favouring them only with a brief smile when they held out a subject to which she was supposed, or accustomed, to contribute. I could see that they, critical as ever, were a little baffled by this. They had expected to assist at the accouchement of whatever transformation Heather was supposed to undergo. Yet she offered them no hints as to the reason why she so suddenly and strikingly appeared to have changed. Indeed, had the conversation not been sufficiently well nourished by the frequent exchanges between Dorrie and her sisters or Oscar and his brother, the atmosphere might have seemed a little charged. When Dorrie was complimented (by me) on her dark blue silk suit, Heather remained silent. When Dorrie explained that she had worried about the colour before buying it ('I hope I did the right thing'), Heather was finally moved to interject, 'You should go in for lighter colours. You wear too many prints.' She then returned to a contemplation of her foot. Dorrie, naturally, was charmed by this show of assurance in her normally pliant daughter. Perhaps she was even charmed by Heather's unilateral declaration of independence with regard to her aunts, for although she was a woman of

35

exquisite humility, she was not unaware that Janet and Rosemary assumed the superiority of mothers whose daughters were safely and successfully married, and regarded her, Dorrie, as something of a failure in this respect. For they immediately conjectured that Heather had 'met' someone. Indeed their usual remark, their Parthian shot, half innocent, half guileful, was, 'Met anyone nice this week?' So delicate was this matter that Heather usually defused it by saying, 'Nobody special,' and accompanied this disclaimer with a smile of such general goodwill that there was little more to be said. But when Janet remarked, 'You look as if you've met somebody nice at last,' Heather replied, 'I meet lots of nice people,' thus affording her mother a moment of glory before she hastened to offer the sherry. For pride, Dorrie knew, went before a fall, and she was not a woman to rely on such slender evidence as a change of appearance. Nevertheless, we all felt that Heather had done something praiseworthy, even if puzzling. It was all the more puzzling in that she made no reference to it. Such was her opacity that she could neutralize all enquiries. It was as if she had overcome, in secret, whatever obstacle had hitherto kept her obediently at home, a daughter to her parents, one whose loyalty would never be in doubt, for there was no occasion on which it had ever been doubted.

With the sherry the discussion turned to holidays. Oscar and Dorrie had a flat on the Spanish coast, near Puerto Banus, and they usually went there at the end of April for a couple of weeks. They so hated leaving home that they never contemplated this visit without a return of their habitual melancholy, and had to be urged into it by their more vigorous relations, all of whom seemed to be anxious to get them there and back as quickly as possible. I actually liked to think of them sitting on their balcony, silently musing on whatever preoccupied them, emerging from this silence only to drink a cup of tea or to eat a thoughtful meal. I imagined them delivered from their leisure only when the sun went down, for although they dutifully paid their respects to it they preferred to withdraw behind the sliding glass doors that would eventually shut them off from the heat and the dazzle and the car horns. Then, in the delivering dusk, they would turn to each other and smile. I imagined Oscar holding out a hand to Dorrie and saying, 'All right, darling?', as if another day's trial had been successfully overcome. Actually, although they went to the flat two or three times a year, I believe they were only happy in their accustomed chairs in Wimbledon. They were at the same time timorous and worldly, yet their preoccupations seemed to remove them from the sphere they so successfully occupied.

'Yes, I expect we shall be off in a couple of weeks,' said Oscar with a sigh, and Dorrie added, as if to comfort him, 'Heather does so love the sun. And she needs it after working so hard all the winter.'

Heather cleared her throat slowly. 'I don't think I'll be coming this time,' she said. 'I don't think I can make it.'

Dorrie and her sisters turned to her as one. 'But, darling,' Dorrie began, only to be interrupted by the aunts. 'But you always go in the spring, dear,' and, 'You love it there. You know you do.' It was Ann, Sam's effete wife, who was never quite in tune with the others, who said, 'Maybe Heather's got other plans this year.' This was felt to be something of an intrusion, yet it was clear that no one was to leave the room until the reason for Heather's curious behaviour had been brought to light. It was again Ann, who always tried so hard and usually so unsuccessfully to keep up with the others, who said, 'I think Heather's met someone at last.'

'Yes, I have, actually,' said Heather indifferently. 'Any more sherry, Mummy?'

With a slightly shaking hand, Dorrie poured her

daughter a second glass of sherry. Her face expressed both delight and terror. The aunts, on the other hand, were disconcerted. That this should have been accomplished without their intervention did not altogether please them. They thought, I am sure, of those little parties at which Heather had so signally failed to shine and which provided them with secret ammunition against their too successful sister, she who had been so backward in youth that they were accustomed to think of her as in need of their patronage.

'Very nice, dear,' said Gerald moderately, for he no doubt saw vistas of conversation waiting for him when he got home, spoiling his evening's television.

'Well, tell us more about him.' This was Rosemary, Lawrence's wife, and the more aggressive of the two. Her tone of voice revealed her to be affronted. There was danger in the air, as there always is when mixed motives come to the surface.

'Oh, I dare say you'll meet him one of these days,' replied Heather, scoring yet another almost invisible victory. 'We'd better go, Mummy, if I'm to drop Rachel off.'

'Are you out tonight, dear?' asked Dorrie. This was still a permitted question, as it was asked every week.

'Yes,' was all Heather would say.

And I, who was to be so summarily dropped off, rather than taken home, began to feel a little superfluous. I think I began to see a time when these childish afternoons, the delight of my all too adult life, would no longer include me. There was no reason why they should, after all. I was there by stealth, for by no stretch of the imagination could I now apply to Oscar in any business capacity, although I think he would have been flattered if I had done so. And if I were no longer needed to guide Heather through life, on what pretext could I possibly be expected to accompany her in whatever lay before her? Heather's future avatars were in no sense

38

dependent on me, as was shown by her performance this afternoon, and the secrecy in which she had matured whatever she had in mind. A part of me – that part of us that never grows up – felt sad, and when I glanced across at Oscar I saw that he felt sad too.

At first I thought this might be an early recurrence of Oscar's habitual melancholy, although it rarely came upon him when his family was gathered safely around him and subject to his anxious hospitality. Indeed it was only the sight of those whom he loved, or perhaps, more importantly, of those whom he knew and who knew him, that ever lifted the veil of inwardness from Oscar's face. That was why he always greeted me so kindly, relieved as he was that someone had arrived to break the spell that seemed to enfold him. And this also explained his mild desire to be of service, even to the extent of going through one's figures and doing all the boring things that had once claimed his attention all day and every day. It seemed to me that since nobody applied to him in this capacity any longer he might feel more lonely, although he was surrounded by family affection. But now that he was inactive professionally, he may have become more dependent on these ties, as if he felt that only they could sustain him. I do not think that I exaggerate. Oscar was bound to suffer more from the great change that had taken place in his circumstances than Dorrie; chasms may have opened beneath his feet for all I know. I had never thought to ask him such a personal question, assuming the mood to be one of delicate but general rejoicing. Now I was shocked to see his face so drawn, as he looked at his daughter, looked to his wife, and then got up and poured another glass of whisky for Sam, and, exceptionally, another for himself.

Of course, I knew all about fathers and daughters and what they are supposed to feel for each other. Heather's lack of ardour in acknowledging the fact that she had met someone may have been inspired by the desire to spare her father embarrassment or discomfort. She was, as I have said, shrewd. Maybe this toneless and passionless announcement was part of her enlightened daughterliness. If so, she was surely to be admired. More than this, she was exemplary, for, by the same token, the aunts had been dealt with and the information made public with commendable lack of excitement. Why then was there not a more general air of happiness? For this great occasion was the fulfilment of everyone's desires, including, presumably, those of Heather herself. This was what all the anxiety had been about, the little stratagems, the utilization of outside help (myself). I think the prevailing emotion was one of sadness that the status quo had changed, suddenly, without warning, admitting of no participation, and, moreover, that our presence in that house, taken so much for granted, might not be any longer required, for we would soon be dispersed, and another household would claim the attention of Oscar and Dorrie and no doubt their attendance on weekend afternoons.

It seemed as though after Heather's announcement all we could do was go home. It had not occurred to me that we should leave so much disappointment behind us. Only Dorrie was happy, the smile on her face eager and without guile. It was she who was the heart of this house, she on whom we all depended. When her attention was withdrawn from us we should all feel bereft. And now she would have much to do, for no one doubted that there would be a marriage. Somehow, in that house, anything less was unthinkable.

We drove home in relative silence. 'I'm awfully glad,' I tried to say, for Heather's calm and assurance were by now so pronounced that it seemed as if the wedding were imminent. 'Sweet of you,' she smiled briefly; the phrase sounded unusually sophisticated for Heather. 'How did you meet him?' I pursued. 'All on my own,'

40

she said, and grinned suddenly, as if acknowledging that she had always known the plots that were being woven around her. 'I met him in the travel agent's when I went to book their tickets to Spain. You'll meet him next weekend, probably. You won't mind going down on your own, will you?'

'I shall miss your parents,' I said, a little timidly. 'And you too, of course. I have loved knowing you all.' For I somehow imagined leave-taking to be in order.

She turned to me with amazement in her face. 'You mustn't think of not seeing them,' she protested. 'They're very fond of you. And they'll want you around more than ever, now that I shan't be seeing so much of them. And of course I shall want you to come and see me, as soon as I'm settled. You're part of the family now.'

I thought that was decent of her. As we drove on I reversed my original estimate of Heather. Perhaps I based my change of heart on the fact that I had never heard her talk so much on one subject before, or so directly. I began to take a mild, comfortably supine interest in a future that would in some measure include myself. In the quiet streets the light had brightened into a weak late sun. A child skipped along in front of us, one foot on the pavement, one in the gutter: Heather sounded her horn to get her out of the way. Somewhere overhead a light plane droned. In the rain-soaked gardens spring had begun in the steady greening of the grass. Already the almond blossom was fading.

'What's his name?' I asked.

'Michael,' she said, and switched on the radio so that we could hear the news from the outside world, paying our dues in that way if in no other.

41

T H R E E

M Y first impression of Michael Sandberg was that he was blessed with, or consumed by, radiant high spirits. My second impression was that a man of such obvious and exemplary charm must be a liar. He broadcast a sort of hilarity which went well with his fair hair and neat figure: he was the same height as Heather, who remained quiet and restrained in his company, as if to allow him the spotlight which she felt must inevitably fall on him. When I entered the Wimbledon drawing-room the following week I found him in the centre of a group of admiring women, for the aunts succumbed immediately and Dorrie had a look of adoration on her face. Given the chance to examine him for a moment, before I was introduced, I judged him to be playing his part well but with slight exaggerations. He was explaining himself, as I suppose he felt called upon to do, and he managed to field all the questions by answering them before they were asked. Thus all embarrassment was avoided, and this tedious *rite de passage* was accomplished with a certain amount of charm. What I felt, I think, in that short moment before I was drawn into the circle, was that perhaps too much charm was being displayed, and that the expressions of rapture that played across his extremely mobile features were perhaps a little premature, a little out of place, and a little excessive compared with the calm restraint emitted by Heather herself. To my mind, they looked already like an old married couple; but it was a married couple of a kind that fatigues onlookers or witnesses. In this couple, it seemed, the husband was destined to play the child, the clown, even the criminal, while it was the vocation of his wife to absorb the high spirits, however aberrant they might become, and to remain watchful, indulgent, and wise, an ancestor to her child-husband.

This impression was the affair of a moment, and over-critical even by my standards. There was something about his expansiveness that made me uneasy, although it was entirely appropriate to the occasion. His very movements were exaggerated: his clothes seemed agitated, as if hard put to contain him. There was a fearful restlessness about him, something florid and opaque, and yet in repose, which he rarely was, he seemed a conventional enough figure. He was a man of middle height, with a thickish body contained in grey flannel trousers, a white shirt, and a blue blazer with gold buttons: he wore an expensive gold watch and a signet ring on the little finger of his left hand. His tie seemed to signify some association or other which I could not hope to understand. His main feature was his hair: conspicuously golden, thick and wavy, hair that is rarely seen on a man once he has passed adolescence. For the rest, his face was an amalgam of undistinguished features, given animation by the ceaseless smile. The eyes, of a rather washed-out blue, were on the small side, but they were fearfully animated. I wondered where the disagreeable impression I had first received when I met his glance had come from. When his smile faded to a reasonable wattage, I could see that he was rather amiable, not too bright, not perhaps very distinguished, not even very grown up, but doing his best in difficult circumstances. He had the air of dreading the spotlight but playing up to it, and he was doing rather well on this occasion. It was not easy for a youngish man (and I should have said he was about thirty) to field the avid questions of a group of middle-aged women, but he was doing his best and managing to please everyone. If he were doing this without much reference to Heather, who sat looking on, with a remote smile on her face, I supposed that this had been agreed between them beforehand.

He was accompanied by his father: I later learned that his mother was dead. The father had none of the captious brilliance of the son, but in his way looked, to my mind at least, equally unreliable. He was a small neat man, with abundant silver hair, and a look of hard-packed but still active flesh about him. Michael addressed him as 'Colonel', and Dorrie, bewildered, did the same, until instructed to call him Teddy. The Colonel acted rather like his son's manager, instructing him to divulge this or that matter, mostly relating to their family enterprise, which I gathered was something to do with the property or travel business. There was necessarily some confusion over this until it turned out that the father managed a chain of time-share apartments abroad, and that he had done so well at this that he had bought into several travel agencies and was something of an expert and also a monopolist in this field. Apparently he was the man to consult if you wanted to live in Spain or Portugal. As the Livingstones already had their place at Puerto Banus I thought this a happy coincidence, designed to bring them closer together, but it appeared that he was already advising them to sell and go somewhere else. I saw Oscar fielding his advice, with a look on his face as remote and as sphinx-like as Heather's. At any rate, the Colonel was easy to get along with, and allowed nothing to deflect him. He was a restless man, a cigar-smoker, a fast talker, the kind who goes down better with women than with men. Yet for all his uningratiating habits, when he looked at his son, which he did frequently, his face was rueful and devoted. I trusted that look.

I could see that Oscar did too, while Dorrie was too excited to calm down into her usual contemplative mode. It seemed to her as if for once she had done the right thing. And her sympathies were engaged by the

44

plight of this couple, who had apparently brought each other up in the absence of a woman to care for them, and whose attachment therefore had a slightly tragic aspect, as if they were now to lose each other to strangers. Indeed, Michael and his father had all the Victorian overtones that should by rights have attached to Heather, for she who had always been so protected was soon to leave the home and the parents who had so protected her. Yet the anxiety of the Colonel and the ardour of his son argued for their greater vulnerability, and this was where Oscar was to play his part, for in the furnishing of those worldly goods which allay anxiety he was by now an expert. I believe there was a great deal of money on the other side as well, but I imagined this being displayed with the sort of lavishness that undermines faith in the seriousness of the commodity, as if it were fool's gold. Spectacular and unconvincing offers were being made – of properties to be lent for holidays, villas on indefinite loan, private beaches – all of which were wide of the mark because I could see that Oscar had no intention of exchanging his little flat, and that if he did he was quite capable of making his own arrangements, although he would now undoubtedly give offence if he did so. There was something of the pools winner about the Colonel: whereas Oscar could never have been mistaken for one. At the same time, there was a mind running on business, so that he would never let an opportunity slip. 'Well, we shall know who to come to,' said either Gerald or Lawrence, rather dazed by this attempt to get them all to move, while either Lawrence or Gerald added, 'Perhaps you could send us some of the literature.' I could see that they were resisting this man, out of a sort of distaste for his volubility, his accessibility. They were both pacific, largely wordless. But Sam, Oscar's brother, was clearly amused by him, and promised to have lunch with him the following week.

While the Colonel was relocating everyone, his son was talking earnestly and in turn to the aunts, and of course to Dorrie. They looked on him with indulgence, and I could see that he had a special rapport with these simple women, women who loved weddings and babies and cherished these matters over and above all others, simply filling in the time disdainfully until mobilized by another wedding. The married state claimed their strongest loyalties, their finest efforts; already their minds were furiously working on the arrangements, which would be argued out in long telephone calls. They could see that they would meet no opposition to their plans from the motherless Michael, the wifeless Colonel, both of whom seemed to be committed to as rapid a marriage as possible. But perhaps they did everything quickly. That was the impression they gave.

Michael and his father got on very well together, and there was indeed something affecting about them, if only because they were also slightly childish. They touched each other a great deal, which I thought was a good sign; men who are frightened of touching usually never learn to do it properly. They punched each other on the arm, or even clasped each other's hands, and I could see that this was how they had been all through Michael's motherless childhood, and that their closeness was surely a matter for congratulation. By this time, my initial impression had rather worn off, and I was in favour of this match, although I was a little surprised by it. I wondered how much Heather and her future husband had in common, for she was so quiet, so unexcitable, that I could not see how they were to get on. As far as I could judge, they were not wildly attracted to each other, for the frequent claspings of the hand that went on were between Michael and his father rather than between Michael and Heather. At the same time, Michael had a sort of sunniness about him which seemed to preclude any baffling depths of character: I thought that was probably just as well, for Heather, despite her shrewdness, seemed to have very little curiosity and might not have much patience with a difficult or troublesome man. While I was watching them, and for obvious reasons I could hardly be included in much of the conversation, I saw that what Heather wanted from this faintly unlikely match was the sort of completeness she had always witnessed in her mother. She would glide from virginity to matronhood with no sense of a change in her condition: she would duplicate her mother, succeed her, and no doubt become the centre of the family circle in her own home, with the full approbation of that mother whom she planned so closely to copy. And why not? The curious thing about this almost sexless arrangement was that it would probably work, for unlike Dorrie and her sisters, who had full confidence in the arrangement, I did not fully trust this marriage as a true marriage. It was just that I somehow felt that each needed the other for private purposes.

Heather, I could see, was already fitting herself for the marital role. As she sat there, motionless and smiling in the midst of this agitated assembly, she looked like the bride in a Breughel painting, as if she were already at her own wedding breakfast. She seemed to have no doubts, any more than Michael did, and this, in view of the rapidity and secrecy of their courtship, seemed surprising. It was her expression that finally convinced us all. Her smile was not luminous or excited, as might have been expected, but replete, turned inwards, almost bored with the ceremony going on around her. When she saw me, she lifted an eyebrow and nodded in my direction, without any sort of alteration in the smile. I came forward then, and kissed Dorrie, who said, 'Oh, Rachel, isn't this exciting? Sit down, dear. We'll have some tea in a moment.' Everything was out of order. I was introduced to Michael and the Colonel as 'Heather's best friend', which I thought a bit of an exaggeration, but as usual I succumbed to the atmosphere, and smiled and nodded myself as if nothing were amiss. Michael wrung my hand and said, 'I know how fond of you Heather is,' which also surprised me, since I didn't see how Heather would ever have referred to me in this way. Then I realized that he would have said this to anyone who purported to be Heather's friend, even if he had never heard of her until this moment. I responded in kind, of course, partly out of goodwill and appreciation for his efforts, and partly because I so much liked being part of the scene, and the idea of being Heather's best friend seemed to guarantee my inclusion in any future festivities. The Colonel gave me a look from which appraisal was not entirely absent. This too surprised me, but there was so much on offer that I responded to all that was going on. I could see that Oscar was notably less transfixed than everyone else; like his daughter, his smile was remote, and perhaps for that reason a little disappointing. Oh, why so sad? Was this merely an effect of his eternal reserve, the fatigue caused by the onslaught of the Colonel's selling technique, or something else, something he had learned about his future son-in-law? Yes, it must be that, for Michael, it seemed, was not the sort of settled businessman he would have chosen but assistant to his father, for whom he 'acted' when the latter's presence was required elsewhere. I could see that this might result in a rather unsettled existence, if he had to go back and forth to Portugal or Spain, but there was no reason why Heather should not accompany him or even play an active part. She knew the region well, and was a good traveller. And Oscar had given her a little property of her own, near to theirs, so there would never be the fatigue of hotels. I could see her, on her terrace, or on her mother's, for Dorrie would undoubtedly spend more time abroad if her daughter were to be there, placidly waiting for the hyperactive Michael to return from whatever deal he had just landed. I could almost hear the tea being got ready, in that hot sun, as the virtues of a settled life were once more being restated. I thought it would all work out very well.

In the course of the afternoon I learned more. The curious name of Sandberg was conferred on them by some slightly complicated ancestry: there was a Danish grandfather, apparently, as well as an Irish grandmother, or possibly two, but I never got this properly worked out, and it was certainly not my place to ask questions. At the same time, the long periods spent in Spain or Portugal had resulted in a very slight blurring of the sibilants in their speech, more noticeable when father and son spoke to each other than when they spoke to the rest of us. It was like a little code between them, rather charming, as was the anxiety with which the Colonel regarded his only child. So deep was the feeling between them that they could only communicate by means of jokes, at which the aunts nodded in slightly bewildered enjoyment. There were more smiles, there was more laughter that afternoon than I could remember before. But I saw that the essential part of these jokes was that not everyone could join in. The unit that the Colonel and Michael formed was a fairly impermeable one. Nevertheless, the sound of their laughter increased the atmosphere of goodwill, and seemed to ensure the happiness of everyone, both now and in the future.

I saw too that I was to be the wedding guest, that, in fact, my function for this family was perceived as quite a positive one. Formerly thought to be the agent of Heather's advancement, I was now to be the reflector of her glory. This did not bother me in the least. I had no romantic views about marriage, or marriages, nor was I consumed with envy. As far as I was concerned, my life was perfectly balanced and satisfying, although I kept

49

quiet about certain aspects of it. Dorrie and her sisters chose to see it as a riot of fun about which I had the good manners to remain discreet, and they had valued my discretion in their desire to promote Heather as the main attraction. My life was not all fun, of course; in fact sometimes it was not much fun at all, but I suppose it suited me. I tried to keep everything within limits, in proportion. I was not made for excess.

Therefore I felt no qualms as I regained my place in this family circle, only too glad to come to rest there. My function was not one that required much of me, either in the way of thought or censorship. I was more than willing to join in these celebrations, except for the worrying idea, that kept coming back to me, no matter how hard I tried to banish it, that something was missing. On the surface all was well. Dorrie, now addressed by the Colonel as 'Dora, my dear', was in a state of such happiness that her eyes frequently had a sheen of tears. The aunts too had smiles of pleasure on their faces, and instinctively turned to their husbands, perhaps laying a hand on a sleeve, or enquiring, with renewed and unconscious tenderness, if they agreed or disagreed with some proposal or other, while the uncles, eased into pleasure by this cessation of restlessness in their wives, responded with more than their usual smiling acquiescence. Even silly Ann, who, I believe, was tolerated but not much liked, failed to give offence, although she kept putting forward tactless questions about the wedding, and this was clearly too big and important a subject to be broached by anyone who was not of the blood, so to speak. Oscar's mouth had relaxed into a smile, and so had his brother's; as they habitually sat side by side, the resemblance was very noticeable. And the atmosphere was decidedly festive, for the married cousins were coming on later to join the party with their husbands, and there were bottles of champagne on ice in the kitchen and tiny

50

smoked salmon canapés already prepared. I understood that Oscar and Dorrie and the Colonel were going out for a late supper somewhere, while Heather and Michael would be going back to Heather's flat to decide which of her belongings and appointments would be needed for their new home. For of course this was to be the occasion for more lavish spending, perhaps the very occasion for which the money had been valued in the first place.

No, what struck me as discordant in this atmosphere of rejoicing was the empty place at the heart of it. I could not, with all the goodwill I was able to summon, see that these two loved each other. I could, of course, see that Heather was capable of, would indeed grow into, a sort of matronly calm, but I thought this impression, which was quite forceful, was rather premature, and I worried that her Gioconda-like smile was a little too placid, a little too immovable. My acquaintance with her (and despite Michael's fervid assurances it was an acquaintance rather than a friendship) had proved her to be uninflammable, but surely she should have been expressing something else beyond her usual detachment, her politeness, her innocence? Surely she should at the very least have been less innocent by now?

The trouble, of course, was her fiancé. I could see that this Michael, this child-husband, was not the sort of man to rouse a woman from the slumbers of virginity, least of all a placid and slow-moving woman like Heather. The impression of ardour that he gave out was to my eyes unconvincing. It occurred to me that he literally did not know what he was undertaking but was if anything responding to his father's needs rather than to his own. I could see that the Colonel's anxiety, expressed in this fast-talking desire to make everyone change place, was in reality for his son, and although there was something heartening about this it also made me uneasy. Why should this anxiety, which seemed to

51

me more maternal than paternal, make itself felt so strongly? Why did the Colonel's eyes never leave his son, or rather why did they return to him after every compliment paid to either Heather or Dorrie? And why did Oscar's eyes never leave him either, when his only child, his much-loved daughter, sat mildly by her mother, having already consigned her future to this man who was not quite grown-up and yet at the same time not quite a real boy, with his golden hair and his blazer and his expensive watch and his adoring father?

I also thought the festive atmosphere a little too Dickensian in its cheerfulness and surprised myself by longing to bring a note of realism into the proceedings. 'Do you know what you are doing?' I wanted to say. 'Do you know what it's all about?' For the couple they formed had something infantile about it, something that irritated me, as I had often been irritated by Heather's sacrificial passivity in the past. And although she had sufficiently emerged from that passivity to have performed the astonishing feat of getting herself engaged to be married, I could not see that she would perform her other duties with the right kind of understanding. For this was where my own experience, extensive, I'm afraid, had kept me from true friendship with Heather. I knew what mattered and she did not. Now I wondered if she ever would and felt that I had grounds for my occasional exasperation with her. Yet I was still disarmed by her kindness. In her slow-moving way she had always been kind, as they were all so kind, as if their kindness were irreversibly bound up with their blamelessness. As if only in a state of complete unknowingness could their marvellous instincts of benevolence and trust have free and full employment. And perhaps Heather had responded to that family conspiracy, that collusion with their own innocence, in her choice of a partner, a partner who would certainly not remove her to an alien world of brutal depths and unwanted rancours. Perhaps even the habitual melancholy of her parents had been adopted in her present stance, for she would surely have grounds for a little secret disillusionment. For she was still very shrewd. But the coalition of innocence and melancholy could be maintained on this basis, and I began to see that it would be.

Things livened up a little when the cousins, Sarah and Georgina, arrived with their husbands, one a doctor, and one a manufacturer of ball-point pens, exactly the kind of go-ahead and self-sufficient young men that Oscar could understand. In comparison with these model husbands Michael's unfocussed radiance appeared even more suspect, but I remembered those dreadful parties to which Heather had been summoned, and for a moment I was almost ready to give my vote to Michael. In any event congratulations were now in order, and everyone but myself seemed to think the omens were good. The cousins were pretty, rather sulky girls who resembled each other. Both had high-pitched exclamatory voices and watchful eyes, and I could see where the slight element of malice that had informed those parties had come from. They were extremely fashionable, and they darted about in their very high-heeled shoes, introducing an independent element of restlessness into this nest of gentlefolk, in addition to the element already present in the person of Michael. Facing up to these new arrivals, Michael almost looked like a man dancing with himself, and his activity was if anything increased when the champagne was brought in. Corks popped, toasts were proposed. 'Michael and Heather!' exclaimed the Colonel, to which Oscar replied, 'Heather and Michael!' The Colonel retrieved his ascendancy by lifting his glass and rallying everyone with, 'Oscar and Dora! New family, new friends. And I hope old friends already.' He then looked at his son, who responded with, 'To Hetty!' He overdid it of course, as if he were already at his own wedding, and this cannibalizing of Heather's name did not go down too well with Oscar, but by now it was too late to rearrange matters, and on that slightly hectic note we all drank deeply, and in my case, and I am sure in Oscar's, thoughtfully. Then I decided that it would be tactful to take my leave of them so that they could have a proper family party without outsiders. Or with only Michael and the Colonel.

I telephoned Dorrie the following morning, a Sunday, and told her what a lovely party it had been. She was childishly grateful for an opportunity to prolong her euphoria and told me all the wedding plans, which had been discussed after I left. Perhaps they all thought I would have minded, would have been smitten with a bridesmaid's gloom, if I had been there. There were to be no bridesmaids, of course. In fact Heather had, with unexpected firmness, stood out against any elaborate fantasies that Dorrie might have been maturing, with the full collaboration of her sisters. 'It's all arranged, Mummy,' she had apparently said. 'We're having a tea-dance.' Once this idea had been mooted, Dorrie began to see its possibilities. 'And it's to be very soon,' she added proudly. 'As soon as we've found her a nice flat, although Oscar's been busy looking for the past week. And he thinks he's found just the thing. He's taking me to see it this afternoon.' I said that everything sounded marvellous. 'Of course, I'm going to be very busy,' she went on. 'But you won't forget me, will you, Rachel? Or Heather? She relies on your judgement, you know. And we shall expect you next Saturday as usual, dear, if you've nothing better to do. You know your way now.'

I warned myself against colluding with this curiously passionless excitement, although it was the very absence of passion, the very even tenor of controlled emotion, that had attracted me to the Livingstones in the first place. It seemed to me now as if their former lives had had a mature calm which had vanished, replaced by a rather more commonplace activity which became them less. Dorrie *affairée* was slightly less attractive to me than the timid and sighing embodiment of domestic immobility, while Oscar the man of property was inferior in my view to the gentle and indeed rueful man who would cast aside his newspaper, smooth down his tie, and greet Heather and myself as if we were still children. My next visit to their house, on the following Saturday, was even slightly nostalgic for those early days of our friendship, which seemed to me now almost prelapsarian, untouched as they were by adult considerations, hermetic, indifferent to the world's events and news. The safety that I had felt in their particular enclosure had evaporated and was replaced by a certain glumness as I was called upon to view the splendour of Heather's appointments. Dorrie had been shopping with a vengeance, meeting her sisters for lunch at the Capital Hotel and going on afterwards with them to plunder the stores, making for Harrods on an almost daily basis. Appalled as I was by the array of saucepans, china, glass, linen, and above all, the glossy nightgowns and dressing-gowns so lovingly purchased by her mother, I did have time to reflect that there was even something age-old and defensible about these preparations, and I imagined the three sisters setting out on their pilgrimage every day, united as they had not been since childhood, or rather since the last wedding. This, they obviously felt, was what women were for. And the sisters were mobilized on Dorrie's account because they had always felt that she was the one most in need of scolding, of supervision. Only in the event of this final marriage, the last child to leave home, would they retain their earlier status; by the same token, a certain amount of deference was due to Dorrie, whose dignity, they

55

felt, was newly conferred upon her by events. The little sister had grown up.

I learned in the course of that fairly distracted afternoon that a flat had been purchased for Heather and Michael in a large block behind Marble Arch. The flat had been newly decorated just before the previous owners had had to leave it, due to a posting abroad, and all that needed to be done was to fill it with furniture of the kind most favoured by the Livingstones. This was now actively under way. Heather, apparently, had no firm views on interior decoration, which I found a little surprising in view of her way with clothes: she was capable of a kind of outlandish chic, which was immediately undersold by her mild, questing expression. She was however quite content to let her mother provide the necessities, and already piles of bath towels, in royal blue, were mounting up next to the enormous range of white French porcelain bowls and dishes, the tomato red casseroles, the electric toasters and kettles, and even the terracotta vases and tubs for their terrace. Vans must have been streaming out of Harrods in convoy. There was something enjoyable about this excess, although I had the feeling that it proceeded more from Dorrie's longing for her child than from the child herself. Heather made a brief appearance on this occasion, with her usual absent-minded expression; none of this seemed to touch her very closely, or perhaps she merely took it all for granted, having had a protected upbringing and a long acquaintance with the world's material goods. The acquisitions were taken far more seriously by Michael, who endeared himself to Dorrie by his grave examination of her purchases. It occurred to me that this wedding must be costing a great deal, but nobody seemed to mind. A fever of spending, a religious ecstasy, had taken hold of Dorrie, and she was not to be diverted. When Heather put in her brief appearance, with the crowd-pleasing Michael in train, all Oscar could say was, 'Go and tell your mother to sit down, will you?' And later, after she had reappeared, in her usual noiseless, undramatic way, his only words were, 'Where's your mother?'

They were to honeymoon in Venice, at the Gritti Palace Hotel. This was the Colonel's contribution, and I felt that he had the more economical part of the alliance. The offers of villas in Portugal or Spain had proved to be illusory, or at least not conclusive, and not to be concluded without a great deal more discussion and display of expertise. I got the feeling that the Colonel had been impressed by the Livingstones' serious attitude to expenditure, and had found himself forced to live up to them. The odd unsaleable villa that he might have had up his sleeve had been returned to its file, and he had risen to the heights demanded of him, even to the extent of arranging a holiday without a discount, without a percentage for himself, or any of those complicated returns that people in the travel business know about. I can't say why I thought of him as mean. He wasn't; and he appeared to be well off. It was just that his money didn't seem to me to be as straightforward as the Livingstones', and wherever it came from or wherever it went to seemed to be hedged about with restrictions. I began to see that Michael's childhood might have been spent in more wearisome circumstances than Heather's, that he might have been aware of his father's affairs, the speculations, the occasional gigantic windfall, the years of affluence, and the periods of bluff. I began to feel sorry for him.

But the wedding was truly charming. I didn't go to the register office – for Heather had, unexpectedly, stood out against a religious ceremony – but merely turned up at the Ritz with my shoes in a paper bag, exactly like a child going to a party. Outside, the rain was streaming down, and for once I didn't mind it, so great was the emanation of festivity from the hotel itself. Inside, the streaming windows merely enhanced the beauty of the white flowers, and through the veil of water I could see the green of the park, now in full leaf. Heather and Michael were wearing deliberately similar white suits, in which they looked young and solemn. Dorrie and her sisters were the ones to do the wedding full honours: silk dresses, large hats, frail sandals. The Colonel and Oscar were in morning dress, the Colonel looking like a bantam as he paraded jauntily up and down the receiving line, his hands clasped beneath the tails of his coat. Oscar greeted me with a smile that was almost weary. He pressed my hand, and said, 'Our little Rachel. Thank you for coming, dear.' I had to turn away, for sudden tears had come into my eyes. Dorrie was so happy that I doubt if she knew who was there. I resolved not to bother her, but to write her a long letter the following day. She would like that.

The idea of a tea-dance was a great success with Heather's friends, those mysterious friends with whom she was reported to have spent her evenings. There were a great many of them, but they were a homogeneous lot; they might all have come from the same family. The dancing got under way pretty early, and the image of the children's party came back to me as the young people took to the floor, while their elders drank tea at little tables and waiters sped round with plates of delicious pastries. There was probably champagne but I didn't come across it. It was when I saw Michael and Heather dancing together, in their white suits, that I began to see that this might not be the empty partnership that I had feared. There was no excitement, no languor in their performance; on the contrary, they looked absorbed, business-like, even slightly careworn, as they foxtrotted round the ball-room. They looked like children, learning to dance on the parquet floor of their dancing school, good children from another age, allowed to amuse themselves to the

58

sound of a wind-up gramophone. They danced all the afternoon, intently, and without conversation. When they eventually decided, by mutual and unspoken arrangement, to go back to the top table, their place was taken by Oscar and Dorrie, who amazed and delighted us all by dancing a perfect tango. There was no doubt in my mind which was the properly married couple. Dorrie, fugitive blushes crossing her face, dipped and turned in as gentle an expression of courtship as I dare say has ever been seen, while Oscar expanded into the man I always supposed him to be, arms masterfully extended, expression with a hitherto unnoticed patina of secret pride and amusement. The floor cleared while they were dancing, and as Oscar bent Dorrie backwards murmurs of admiration arose from the younger couples, who had only ever seen this sort of thing on television. Her feather-patterned blue silk trailing momentarily on the floor, Dorrie was abruptly swung upright, and as the dance ended and everyone applauded they both smiled shyly and clasped each other's hands. It was delightful.

I had to leave before the end. As I turned to go I looked back and saw, against a background of vague green and streaming windows, Heather and Michael, in their white suits, dancing on and on, sturdily quickstepping round the floor, and quite impervious to the romance of the occasion. It seemed very quiet in the lobby. I changed my shoes in the ladies' room, and went out into the rainy street, suppressing a shudder at the wet needles that fell on my head, and bracing myself to stand at the bus-stop with all the other wage-earners, still hearing the strains of the tango in my mind, and still seeing those two children, white-suited, dancing to their wind-up gramophone, while the rain streamed down and drowned all the white flowers.

F O U R

AFTER this I found myself in rather a lull. Heather and Michael were in Venice, and Oscar and Dorrie were recuperating from the wedding in Spain. We were busy in the shop and I was fairly tired in the evenings, too tired to seek very far for entertainment. Robin, my colleague, saw me languidly gathering my things together at the end of a hectic Saturday afternoon and said, 'What you need is more exercise.' I should explain that Robin copes with his life extremely well by belonging to a lot of clubs: health clubs, jazz clubs, theatre clubs, and so on. He is a frequenter and a discoverer of wine bars. A mild but organized bachelor in his mid-thirties, he has solved the problem of leisure by being out all the time. In this way he is able to both leave and find his flat immaculate and undisturbed, and the low-level degree of companionship seems to suit him very well. He is one of those men who says, 'I am never lonely' (though I suspect he is), and, 'London satisfies all my needs'. When he takes his holiday he goes on package art tours of Italy or walks, with a party set up for this purpose, in the Lake District. He maintains that his extremely consistent output of work and concentration is assured by his habit of jogging every morning and swimming at his health club every evening once the shop is closed.

Robin is the only person who knows about my fear of water, and he is constantly urging me to go swimming with him. 'It's just a matter of getting used to it,' he said to me, seeing me drooping in the back of the shop, 'and the benefits are enormous. And psychologically you'll be a different person. Look at me. I used to have colds all the time. Now I'm a hundred per cent fit.' He still has colds, but I didn't point this out. 'You can come with me this evening,' he went on. 'There'll be nobody there. And I won't watch if you don't want me to. You don't have to dive or anything. Just get in and swim a few lengths. You'll be a different person,' he repeated.

The different person I was going to be (for we all want to be different) did in fact accompany him that evening. It is hard to describe how or what I felt. I was a good swimmer because we had lived by the sea when I was small, and my father and I had swum almost every morning in the fine weather. Besides, it was not swimming that I was afraid of. I think it was actually the sight of water and some vague but powerful fear of being sucked into it. When I had walked into the sea with my father I had felt quite safe, but, undressing at Robin's health club, I could hear the peculiar muted din of water being violently disturbed and I began to shiver. Standing on the edge of the pool I could see a little steam hovering over the chemical chlorinated blue, and below me a pattern of tiles wavering and shifting; my leg, when I inserted it, immediately looked blanched and dead. A man wearing goggles and a nose clip was ploughing furiously up and down, and I was fearful of the commotion he was setting up, of the mess and foam he was creating. The noise echoed under the glass roof, a mournful and reverberant noise that filled me with horror. I waited until he was out of the way before launching myself and managed to swim a length without much trouble. But he was faster than I was or wanted to be, and I could hear him behind me. Every so often he passed me, rocking me in his wake; once my nostrils filled with the waves made by his arms and I retreated to the side, coughing in a hysteria of fear. 'Go on,' shouted Robin. 'Don't give up.' Two girls, of enviable slimness, watched me curiously, before losing interest and neatly up-ending themselves in the water. They came up, hair streaming, and turned on their backs and floated. Water to them was familiar, an element in which they could play; their streaming hair made fronds below the surface. They decided to race each other, backstroke, and at one point, caught between their flailing arms and the man in the goggles, I thought I must sink. I couldn't, of course; I was too good a swimmer, but my mind seemed to give way. I felt I must surrender, break down. I wanted no more of it. I waited for a gap and swam to the side; when I got out, my legs were shaking. Even when I was dressing I could hear the dull shouting, magnified under the glass roof, and the fact that these were sounds of enjoyment made no difference to me. I knew that I had not beaten my fear, that I never should, and I resolved never to put myself to this needless test again. I should simply avoid all expanses of water. I did not feel I had to prove anything. Or rather, I had just proved something. My fear was still there.

That night I slept heavily, the sleep of exhaustion, or of regression. 'There you are, you see,' Robin said to me the following Monday. 'I told you you could do it.' I said nothing, for it was not his fault, was not even anything to do with him. But the incident had thrown me off balance and I was rather thoughtful for a while.

The process of thinking does not become me. I feel my face growing longer, my eyes sinking deeper. Thinking, for me, is accompanied by a wave of sadness. Therefore I try to avoid introspection. I long ago decided to live my life on the surface, avoiding entanglements, confrontations, situations that cannot quickly be resolved, friendships that lead to passion. With my quite interesting work, and the affairs that I keep quiet about, I reckon I manage pretty well. I tend to be rather merciless with those of my friends who cannot do the same, and I favour sensible arrangements. I dream a lot, and apart from my dreams of drowning, I like and value the night hours, when I seem to be in an altered state.

62

Then I am able to tolerate myself. In the daytime I keep busy, always on the surface, and that suits me too. Sometimes I meet someone who makes me think that I might always be as I am in my nocturnal imaginings: dreamy, vulnerable, childish. The Livingstones fulfilled this function for me. After being grown-up and liberated throughout the week I could regress comfortably and safely in their welcoming and uncritical presence. They were not bound to me by ties of blood, nor even of affinity: they made no demands, did not suggest ways in which I might improve myself or change my life. No one thought I ought to move from my flat above the shop or go on holiday or do anything energetic and uncharacteristic. They were not inquisitive about my habits or relationships, did not expect me to do anything except turn up on a fairly regular basis and assist at the unrolling of their noiseless and curiously unhopeful lives. This I was more than willing to do. In exchange for my presence and my interest, always unfeigned, they offered the seduction and the novelty of a fixed point, one that drew me on like a charm, perhaps because of the deliberate lack of fixity in my own perspectives. I did not even have to say much when I was with them, but could drift contentedly on the stream of their desultory talk, could annihilate my daytime self, and merely be present in the body, waking from time to time to scrutinize their undemanding presence. The fact that they revealed nothing of their inner lives was an added pleasure of their company. I had no doubt that their inner lives were as complicated as my own (but I had made a conscious decision to eschew complications) or indeed as anyone else's; from their withdrawn expressions I assumed them to be living at some subterranean level, immersed in a sea-dream that never rose to the surface. Their sleepwalking demeanour, the food that always appeared as if by magic, and the abundance of material goods that flowed

63

through their lives I took to be signs of a fortunate dispensation. I grudged them nothing, I envied them nothing, merely rejoicing in the aspect of their successful arrangements with fate. Their forays into the outside world heartened me, marked as they were by even greater abundance, but it was the deep peace and safety of their home, rooted and furnished and nourished as it was, that drew me to them, drew me on into deeper acquaintance. When I was not with them I rarely thought of them, for they made no calls on my time. We practically never telephoned each other, except for the excitement of the engagement, when calls were more frequent, for we had nothing much to say. I had simply been gathered in, and my justification was that I would bear some vague responsibility for Heather, always to my mind the least capable of them all at looking after herself in this cruel world, always absent, always in need of care. Now it seemed as if she too had been gathered in, and I began to wonder, rather sadly, if I should be needed any more.

So that I was all the more glad, after about a month, to receive a telephone call from Dorrie. They were back from Spain, and Heather and Michael were due to arrive from Venice that evening. Would I care to join them for tea the following day at Heather's flat? She was sure that Heather would like to see me. 'And of course we've missed her. And Michael too, of course. I'm taking some food over – she'll be too tired to do anything for a while. You know how to find the flat, don't you, Rachel? We'll see you there about four, then.'

It was clear to me from this conversation that Dorrie had no idea of the reality of her daughter's marriage, but had simply thought in terms of the wedding. If she considered it at all, she conceded that marriage might have 'tired' Heather, as if she had been subjected to repeated assaults from her husband. Privately, I assumed this to be an impossibility. I had an image of

64

the golden-haired Michael in his white suit and his bride in hers and of their nursery-style dancing and of his ghastly father, and if I knew anything at all it was that theirs was some peculiar but no doubt satisfactory arrangement, agreeable to them both, whereby they removed themselves from parental care and oversight and played at being grown-ups. As far as I could see, no deep feeling, indeed no feeling at all, had come into play. Heather's rather bovine expression had not changed at all throughout this adventure. As for Michael, he had had to be prompted by his father, as if, left to himself, he might forget the whole thing. The Colonel's anxiety I now tended to interpret as a partly justified fear that without his supervision this marvellous alliance might slip from his grasp. This anxiety, which, even at the time, I had thought almost maternal, was what a mother with a particularly lack-lustre or indeed frankly impossible daughter might feel on seeing the perfect opportunity of disposing of her with honour about to fade from her grasp. Michael, I thought, was negligible. Michael was a son: he would never be a husband. Did he know what husbands were like? What they did? He had never seen his father behave like one, for his mother had died at his birth. I had no doubt that the Colonel had had a few little arrangements of his own, for I remembered that look of appraisal he had bestowed on me; at the same time, I knew somehow that these arrangements had been conveyed to his son in a mixture of bluster and subterfuge, with knowing looks and laughter to which the boy would try to adapt himself, only gradually growing into an understanding of what this meant. At the same time I knew that Michael's answering laughter would conceal distress, would keep him frozen in childhood bewilderment. For this reason I hoped that Heather's shrewdness would be sufficient to cope with the situation.

And they had danced together like brother and sister.

65

That was what had worried me at the time. It even worried me slightly now, although I began to feel my familiar exasperation with Heather, as I always did just before seeing her, as if the sight of her mild face stimulated me to a fury both on her account and on my own. Well, if she were either stupid enough or clever enough – I could never decide which – to enter into a *folie à deux* with this strangely affecting and disappointing man, that was surely her own affair. It was certainly nothing to do with me, although I began to see that at some point she might run into trouble. But I remembered her extreme reticence, the way she had issued news of her courtship in the form of a single bulletin, almost a press statement, the competent way with which she had dealt with the enquiries of her aunts, and I assured myself that she knew what she was doing. I was all the more anxious to believe this because I did not relish the task of lining up my experience with Heather's inexperience and taking on the burden of inducting Heather into a fully adult life. In a way I wanted Heather to remain as she was, just as I wanted Oscar and Dorrie to remain as they were, fixed points in a volatile universe. I simply wanted things to go on as they were, an unchanging backdrop against which I could conduct my own variations. I saw them as the dry land to which a hapless swimmer such as myself might cling for safety.

I dare say everyone has arrangements of this kind, little bargains struck with uncharacteristic activity or behaviour. Eileen Somers, from my shop, a widow with two undergraduate sons, has a side-line in free-fall parachuting. Her late husband was a Wing-Commander in the Royal Air Force, and she feels that in this way she can keep in touch with him. Eccentricities abound in the most orthodox, the most humdrum of lives. And who was I to criticize this marriage that had been launched in the most genial of circumstances, with the almost frenzied goodwill of both sets of parents? For the parents had, on both sides, every reason to wish to see their offspring settled. Perhaps I sensed that there was some reservation as to how these children might be inducted into real life that gave me pause, or perhaps it was Oscar's thoughtfulness when he scrutinized Michael that worried me. But in the end it was hardly my affair. I left the shop to Robin and Eileen and set out to walk to Marble Arch, determined to enjoy my rôle as spectator, determined also not to involve myself in matters regarding an intimacy which I had no desire to share.

It was a bright windy day in early June. The summer had not been a good one so far. Brisk south-westerlies had kept the temperature down, and there seemed to be road-works everywhere. Dust blew into my eyes as I walked along Notting Hill Gate into the Bayswater Road, where Japanese tourists gazed uncomprehendingly at the junk displayed against the railings of the park. Doomed as they were to walk about all day, it was possible to feel for them an immense compassion. I was glad that summer journeyings were not for me. I usually went away after Christmas, in the slack season, thus allowing Eileen and Robin to get on with their action-packed lives. I never minded summer in the city and frequently wandered about in the evenings after the shop was closed. I liked the feeling that everyone was abroad and that London was inhabited by transients. Sometimes I wandered long and far, and only returned home after nightfall. So far I had not done so this year, but the return of the Livingstones signified that I was in some way free once more, as if their rootedness gave me the security to be rootless, to test my vagrancy against their stability, my preparedness for adventure against their bourgeois world. The contrast was perhaps necessary to me for reasons which were present in me, not as reasons, but perhaps as instincts, as if I and they existed to offset each other in a way to benefit both conditions, as if I, in my willed impermanence, could look to them to measure it, and as if they, sensing this, looked to me to provide them with some entry into a region of greater understanding. 'Rachel is a feminist,' Dorrie had once said proudly, introducing me to one of the aunts. I think she thought me very brave. I think they all did.

I found Heather's block of flats behind Norfolk Square, a complex of buildings with a Thirties-ish appearance, curved metal windows catching the afternoon sun. A porter reading the *Daily Telegraph* behind a small desk informed me that the Sandbergs were on the fourth floor. I walked across an expanse of Jazz-Age carpet to a flight of stairs with a chrome handrail, until recalled to order by the porter who indicated the lift: small, but with bronze-coloured doors which slid into one another at the touch of a button. I could smell the Colonel's cigar before I even rang the bell of Heather's flat; he must have preceded me in the lift. I found echoes of his presence distasteful, reminding me of the urgency with which he had previously behaved. But it was Dorrie who came to the door, flustered and happy, and who, after a kiss, ushered me into a Nile green drawing-room where I saw Heather sitting on one of those sofas that have the arms lashed to the back by ropes. Clearly, the decorating here had been done by Dorrie. Other notable features of the room were an oval mirror in a gilt frame surmounted by an eagle (possibly an item intended to underline Michael's masculine presence) and several armchairs of extraordinary depth, with footstools covered in the same pale green silk: elaborate curtains in more of this material were swathed and swagged at the long French windows, one of which was open on to a terrace. The room was in fact rather handsome, and certainly luxurious. Fine china cups and saucers covered with a pattern of little birds stood ready on a piecrust table in front of a fireplace in which a gas fire, simulating live coals, was lit, for it was only intermittently warm, and the windows were soon shut, perhaps as much to emphasize the hermetic closeness of the gathering as for any real reason. Dorrie was obviously longing for it to be dark so that she could light all the lamps with their coral and peach coloured shades. It was the room of a child of the middle classes, one who had never known the austerity, the poverty or the ugliness of an unhappy home. It was also a little out of date, as if fashions which had come and gone had no purchase here, and only the solidity of a conventional bourgeois comfort had any meaning. The air was warm and scented with Dorrie's muted honeysuckle cologne. Although I had just arrived, she had already darted out of the room, and tinkling noises announced the preparation of tea. It was clear that she was duplicating her own rituals, with no sign of an interruption, barely acknowledging the fact that her daughter was in charge of this establishment, with its elegant appointments and its air of sophistication. She seemed delighted to be doing the honours, and Heather in her undemonstrative way was apparently pleased that she should. In fact Heather was so extremely immobile that I wondered briefly if she might be pregnant. Since she had only been married a month, and since her husband was nowhere in sight, nor was there any trace of him in the room, I dismissed this possibility from my mind. In any event it didn't fit in with my theory.

There were only four of us, Oscar, Dorrie, Heather, and myself. The men, Dorrie explained, had had some business to discuss and had gone to the Colonel's office; they would be back later. Over the rim of my teacup I studied Heather. Her expression indicated that nothing was different; nevertheless there were some subtle changes which had, however, entirely to do with the influence of Italy on her always variable garb. 'Did you have a nice holiday?' I asked. (Holiday, rather than

honeymoon, seemed to me to be the appropriate word.)
'Yes, thanks,' she replied. I was grateful to her for not
showing off but felt that probably her reticence was due
to the presence of her parents, particularly of her father,
rather than to my own. Oscar, leaning back full-length
in his engulfing chair, seemed to me to be slightly older,
a little less spruce, than when I had last seen him, but the
shadow of melancholy had temporarily disappeared
from his face. Presently he was mobilized to fit an
adaptor to one of the numerous lamps, for the conveni-
ences of this flat, its commodities even, seemed to be the
sole preoccupation of the elder Livingstones, as if their
son-in-law were incapable of looking after them himself, or, more probably, as if they judged his status to be
too honourable for them to ask him to descend into
practicalities. He disappeared from the room, only to
reappear a few minutes later. 'I'll have to go down to the
shops, darling,' he said to Dorrie. 'I should find something still open. This doesn't fit.' 'Edgware Road,'
Heather offered from the sofa. 'On the corner.' Oscar
looked at her, and for a tiny second hesitated. 'I shan't
be long,' he assured Dorrie. And to Heather, 'Try to get
your mother to sit down.' But Dorrie was already piling
cups on to a tray. 'I'll just wash these,' she said. 'I expect
you two girls want to be alone anyway. You've probably got a lot to talk about.'

The fact that we had never had much to talk about
had completely escaped her. I suppose she thought that
we had intense and intimate conversations in the privacy
of Heather's car and was too modest ever to enquire
about them. In any event there was a silence after she
had left the room and it occurred to me that the
afternoon was going less well than I had expected, or
perhaps was proving less of a treat. I had expected a
renewal, or perhaps even a continuation, of that unthinking, almost soporific, warmth that I usually so
enjoyed in the Livingstones' house, and instead every-

thing was being slightly but noticeably mismanaged. Only Dorrie seemed to think that nothing was wrong, that everything was splendid, that all the omens were favourable. Heather herself seemed less overwhelmed by her good fortune, but then she was always fairly expressionless. 'Well, how have you been?' she enquired finally, but with that benevolent smile she had inherited from her father. 'Oh, I'm all right,' I said. 'How about you?'

'Fine, fine,' she said.

I judged the fact that she had used two words instead of one to be a good sign.

'Not looking forward to going back to work, though,' she added.

'Will you keep on the shop?' I asked, in some surprise.

'Of course,' she said, looking at me with the same surprise. 'Why not?'

'I thought you might find you had to do more at home,' I said lamely.

'Well, no, not really,' she said. 'He'll be travelling quite a bit, you see. And Mummy filled the freezer while we were away. There's nothing for me to do. Anyway, I should be lost without the shop. I've built it up quite a bit. You've never seen it, have you?'

I reminded her that we usually met at her parents' house, for which I already felt nostalgic.

'Well, you must look in and see me. And you're always welcome here, of course.'

She smiled, again with that faint but irresistible kindness, to which I always responded. I think it was that smile, which they all shared, that bound me to them.

I was however a little disheartened. She seemed to me to have passed into another age group, one in which material certainties are taken for granted, romantic love is a thing of the past, and work has assumed the central position that it usually occupies in truly adult lives. I felt, in comparison with this surprisingly assured Heather, a trifle forlorn, as if my life had yet to reach the point at which hers had apparently come to rest. And yet there was no marked change in her. Her hair had grown a little fuller, perhaps, and she was quite conventionally dressed in a rather striking violet print skirt with a thin violet sweatshirt, obviously Italian. Perhaps she had a little more chic, a little more style. If so, it was commendably understated, which I also put down to the influence of Italy. It struck me that she might have some flair in the fashion business after all. 'I bought some marvellous things in Italy,' she added, as if to bear out my assumptions.

That seemed to be the end of our conversation, and I was quite glad when Dorrie came back into the room. 'I expect Rachel would like to see round the flat,' she said to Heather. I got to my feet with a show of alacrity, although my curiosity seemed to have evaporated. I remember noting the bedroom as a cold blue room with one wall taken up by a range of white fitted wardrobes, and an immense bed covered by a pale blue satin counterpane. It looked icy and unused, and I wondered how she could bear it. There were none of Michael's things scattered around, and by now his absence was rather noticeable. And yet I was the only one who noticed it. 'Lovely,' I managed to say. 'You must have worked awfully hard to get it finished so quickly.' 'Oh, the parents saw to everything,' Heather said. 'Most of the stuff didn't arrive until after the wedding. They stayed here for a bit while we were away.'

I reminded myself that there was nothing necessarily unusual about this, although the image of that icy bedroom followed me back into the drawing-room, and I went to the fire to warm my hands. Something had been lost. But, 'Lovely,' I said again, this time to Dorrie. She was already pouring sherry from a square cut–glass decanter. 'Here you are, Rachel,' she said, handing me a glass. 'Now, tell us what you've been doing.'

'Well, we've been quite busy,' I began, but at that moment the front door opened and shut and an aroma of cigar and a volume of subdued but busy talk heralded the arrival of Michael and the Colonel, whom I must remember to call Mr Sandberg, for he was not a Colonel, nor had he ever been one. The title was some impenetrable joke forged in Michael's childhood and perpetuated ever since. Nevertheless he was not averse to using it, and I suppose it suited him well in business. On second thoughts I decided to retain it. For some reason I didn't want to get on the wrong side of him.

They brought with them a bustle and an air of good cheer that struck me as semi-professional. It seemed essential to them always to be laughing, as if without this activity their spirits might plummet to zero or disappear altogether.

'Hello, hello,' exclaimed the Colonel. 'How lovely to see you.'

I doubt if in that instant he had any idea who I was, but his eyes focused and hardened as he looked at me.

'You remember Rachel, don't you, Teddy? Heather's friend?'

'Of course,' he said, retaining my hand, and even squeezing it rather hard. 'I never forget a face.'

'Rachel!' said Michael, having been given the help he needed. 'You look wonderful! How are you?'

I replied that I was fine. I was rather taken aback by this evidence of goodwill, and also by the fact that the entrance of Michael and the Colonel actually eased the atmosphere. Their manufactured *bonhomie* had the effect of putting women at ease, or at least permitting them to behave naturally, perhaps with an element of annoyance, or even bad temper. This at least was the effect they had on Heather, who sighed, 'Do sit down.

73

You make the place look untidy.' She did not seem much affected by the entrance of her husband, who immediately bounded to the sofa, along the back of which he laid one careful arm. The Colonel, cigar clamped between his teeth, was wrestling with the cork of a bottle of champagne which he had brought with him.

'Why, Teddy, what a lovely idea!' said Dorrie, who was now turning on all the lights.

'Well, I thought their first night in their new home,' he explained, as the champagne foamed over the neck of the bottle and dribbled into an ashtray hastily tendered by Dorrie.

'Second,' pronounced Heather from the sofa.

'What was that, dear?' he asked, removing the cigar which he placed in the damp ashtray, where it smouldered disgustingly before Dorrie, with an apologetic murmur, took it away.

Once again I got the impression that the parents were in charge and that the children were under escort. No one was better at giving this impression than Michael, who seemed to rely on the presence of his father for effective functioning. Heather, I sensed, might turn mutinous in time, although she too had a tremendous tolerance of parental interference. I looked at her, sitting stolidly on the sofa, drinking the champagne which made no appreciable difference to her mood, and at her husband, who was tossing peanuts and tiny cheese biscuits into his mouth like a dog, or a very small child.

'Here, here,' said the Colonel, lighting another cigar. 'Don't eat all those. What about Rachel?'

'Sorry, sorry,' he said, brushing crumbs on to the floor, and offering me a depleted dish. 'Lovely to see you, Rachel,' he repeated, and winked.

It was not quite clear to me why he thought we should be in such complicity. I got up to leave, for I found the atmosphere ambiguous, and rather a strain.

'Not going already, are you?' said the Colonel. 'We can't have that.'

He was one of those men who think they are good at getting women to change their minds, but I had no trouble in dealing with this. Men of his age like to think they are masterful, whereas their chief attraction, did they but know it, is that they only have power over material necessities. To people of my generation they appear quite toothless. I had no doubt that in the ballrooms of his youth the Colonel had been noted for his charm and his way with women. It was a style which he had carefully taught his son, who had never, as far as I could remember, uttered a serious word. Badinage was obviously the favoured means of exchange in the Sandberg establishment. Part of me could not bear to watch the ruined child I took Michael to be, or to imagine the efforts he would have to make to live without his father's supervision. Heather I thought the more down to earth of the two, but in her way equally enigmatic.

I kissed Dorrie, who made disappointed noises, shook the Colonel firmly by the hand, and said to Heather, 'Would you both have dinner with me one evening? I'll book some theatre tickets. Think of something you'd like to see and let me know.' They both looked childishly pleased at this, and I felt almost moved by their pleasure. I seemed to be on the verge of several emotions, an interesting but uncomfortable combination of boredom and sadness, regret too. I realized with a pang of pity that it could not have been easy for Heather and Michael to behave naturally under all this scrutiny. I was almost indignant on their behalf at the continued presence of their parents, although they themselves took Dorrie and the Colonel as an entirely natural component of their communal lives. Poor Oscar, who must still be patrolling the Edgware Road, was no doubt more alive to the potential difficulties of the situation but was too careful of Dorrie's happiness to try to stop her in her efforts to create a home from home for her only child. Perhaps she thought that Heather would be lonely without her. As I say, she was a very innocent woman.

I met Oscar on the stairs when I was leaving, my hand skimming along the chrome handrail as I ran down, anxious to be gone. I was aware of his patient tread before I saw his mild eyes lifted up to mine.

'Going already?' he asked, but he did not seem surprised. He, despite his efforts, was the least happy of them all. 'Don't abandon us, Rachel, now that Heather's gone,' he said.

This was strange; both he and Dorrie had made this remark at various times and in different situations. Besides, I thought their function was not to abandon me. But I suppose they saw me as one who might, if needs be, negotiate a passage for them, someone sturdy, streetwise, on their side. And I think that Oscar still had reservations about Heather's fate. I did not, however, see that I had any further part to play in this, and had indeed found the afternoon disappointing, even slightly disturbing. But I assured Oscar that they would see as much of me as they could stand, and told him that I had asked Heather and Michael for an evening on their own. At this the heaviness lifted from his face, and he pressed my hand in gratitude. I left him, with his adaptor, and a bunch of roses which he had been unable to resist, standing on the stairs and looking after me. His patient face came back to me at various odd moments during the evening, and for some reason I imagined him, a suppliant, with his roses, outside his daughter's door.

F I V E

NEVERTHELESS, it seemed as if our friendship might have reached a natural conclusion, might be at an end. It occurred to me that we really had little in common. I had comforted myself, falsely, I now saw, with the illusion that these people might function as a family for me. Now I saw that they existed only for each other. The horrible thought struck me that all the time that I had been intent on appropriating them for my own purposes, they were in reality sorry for me. This idea, oddly enough, had never struck me before, probably because they were so genuinely kind, so very sensitive and delicate. Yet now that it had entered my consciousness I could not get rid of it. My secret life, and what Dorrie referred to, and no doubt thought of, as my feminism, cannot have struck them with anything but with pity. They dealt in euphemisms, and while describing me as brave, felt on my behalf all the deprivations of which I was hardly conscious, having lived with them for most of my adult life. I now saw that I had succumbed rather too readily to the enticements of their existence, and that they had noted this. I also was in no doubt that the arrangement between us could continue for as long as I wished it to, for they were genuinely fond of me, and they still thought of me as a friend of their daughter, and a friend for their daughter in case anything should happen to either of them. They were blameless people, good people, and yet I knew that they had somehow earmarked me as a subordinate, someone who might step in and continue their guardianship in due course. This did not bother me. But the idea behind the assumption did. It was as if they knew that my emancipation would lead inevitably to lifelong spinsterhood, and that in this capacity (or incapacity, according to their thinking) I would be available for, no, grateful for, any function that would give me a purpose in life.

This idea struck me as rather amusing, although it had a certain painful aspect to it. It was undeniable that I knew more about the ways of the world than Heather, but as far as I was concerned she had only to do her homework in order to catch up with me: the onus was on her, and I certainly did not intend to be on hand to guide her. With the wealth of material goods at her disposal, with all the necessities of life supplemented by all of the luxuries, she had little left to do with her time except cultivate her feelings, and if these feelings, properly cultivated, brought a certain amount of disillusionment in their train I did not see that it was my responsibility to cushion the blows for her. She had chosen a defective husband, that I could see; but on the other hand he might be the instrument, the chosen agent, of her long delayed maturity. I thought of those two children in their slightly overblown apartment – such a contrast to my own deliberately underfurnished rooms – and I decided to let them get on with it. I would proffer my invitation in due course, but I would not be in any hurry. And if they should by any chance think of me, I would maintain a slightly offhand stance. I would not in any circumstances urge my attendance on them. And with their curiously inert attitude to life, I doubt that they would even notice my absence.

Towards Oscar and Dorrie I felt differently. Realizing that they might in secret, and so discreetly, have commiserated over my prospects, I felt a certain amount of hurt and indignation, which I quickly converted into the sort of impatience that comes over one with the realization that a love affair is going badly and that it would be better to end it. I am good at cutting my losses, as many people have found out in their time. But despite all my efforts I still thought of them kindly and with respect; I even thought of them with nostalgia for the whole picture of their lives, which they conducted in a sort of lost paradise of unworldliness that was very far from anything I knew, or with which I had contact. I still found myself thinking of them, and constructing their habits around them: I remembered little things like the pattern of their teacups, or Dorrie's reported shopping expeditions, or the way the aunts dressed up for their Saturday afternoon visits. I remembered with astonishment their tranquil investment in the things of this world, as if they thought they were going to live for ever, but at the same time the wistfulness with which they regarded each other, as if they really knew that one of them would die first. What would happen then? Would Heather be up to the task of comforting and sustaining? Would anyone? Who could be a parent to those parents when the time came, when that Biblical day arrived and the silver chord, the golden bowl, revealed their essential fragility? Love, which they had never lacked, surrounded them like a haze of sunlight; they were not made for the dark, as some of us are. Love had made them vulnerable, only able to seek and find each other. And was this condition, which I saw as inherently painful, the reason why their daughter had deliberately chosen its opposite, thus permitting herself to rest secure in the knowledge that she would never suffer abandonment, dereliction, infidelity, bereavement? I had always thought her shrewd, and I saw her now as very much her father's daughter. Where's your mother? I heard, or seemed to hear, Oscar's question, which meant so much more than it was designed to mean, as if he feared that the object of his love were eternally about to disappear, as if he might then embark on some mythic quest to bring her back. Thus Heather, saving all her strength in this unrealistic and insignificant marriage of hers, might at last find herself called upon to play her part, having perfected herself in secret for this purpose. For I knew for a fact that Dorrie would die first.

An unpleasant thing happened around that time. I was sitting in my flat one evening, wondering whether to go out or stay in, when the telephone rang. Most of my friends were out of town and I did not recognize the voice, which sounded brisk and sporty.

'Rachel? Hallo, my dear. Just wondered how you were.'

'I'm sorry. Who is this?'

There was a sort of chuckle at the other end. 'Come on, now. You can't have forgotten me already.'

'I'm sorry,' I said again. 'Who is this?'

Another chuckle. 'A friend of yours. Or rather someone who would like to be a friend. You look like a girl who could be a very good friend.'

A terrible realization came upon me. 'Is that Colonel Sandberg?'

The voice became brisker. 'Got it in one. How about meeting me for a drink? The Churchill suit you? Half an hour?'

'I'm so sorry,' I said again, rather carefully. 'I was just going out. So sorry. Goodbye.'

I put down the telephone, picked up my bag, and went out for a very long walk. I didn't get back until it was quite dark. After that, I made a habit of being out in the evenings – I knew he wouldn't telephone in the daytime – thus giving him time to cast his nets elsewhere. The fact that it would be difficult or unwise to face him for a bit was an additional reason for staying away from the young Sandbergs for a little while. The situation was becoming overburdened with restrictions.

I took to walking, therefore, in those late summer evenings. I was disgusted, not in any puritanical or moralistic sense, but because I felt that my life was perhaps a little adrift. If someone as horrible as the Colonel had found me out, then I had to know that something was wrong. And yet I would defend myself. It seemed to me that I conducted my life on rather enlightened principles; that is to say, I imposed certain restraints on my feelings, kept a very open mind, rather despised those conventions that are supposed to bring security, and passed lightly on whenever I saw trouble coming. I had resolved at a very early stage never to be reduced to any form of emotional beggary, never to plead, never to impose guilt, and never to consider the world well lost for love. I think of myself as a plain dealer and I am rather proud of the honesty of my transactions. After all, I have had to make my way in the world, and I could only do so by being clear-eyed and self-reliant. I forbid myself to remember that it has not always been easy, and I never, ever, blame my parents: that sort of thing is so old hat. I pass lightly through life, without anguished attachments, and this was nearly always the way I intended it to be. I say nearly always because I do sometimes have these odd dreams. The dreams are of no interest in themselves, but they leave me wondering where they came from. In dreams I bear children, sink smiling into loving arms, fight my way out of empty rooms, and regularly drown. I wake up in a state of astonishment, and sometimes of fear, but I banish the memory of the dreams, of which no one knows anything. Telling dreams, like blaming one's parents, or falling in love and making a fool of oneself, comes into my category of forbidden things.

And yet the ghastly Teddy, who was obviously even more used to this kind of thing than I was, but fortunately rather out of date, had singled me out. I felt almost ashamed until I realized that he was one of those old-fashioned men who think that a liberated woman is fair game and that she will only want a little masculine attention in order to turn back thankfully into the unreconstructed model. He probably thought he was being rather kind. Had I accepted his invitation I should no doubt have been subjected to a certain amount of propaganda, the same propaganda he had been using all his life in order to get women to change their minds, but virtuously backed up by a desire to make me see the light. Seduction to him would always be disguised as conversion, and I had no doubt that somewhere along the primrose path he would utter the words, 'There's a good girl!' For with his grey conscience, he would look for easy conquests and turn them to good account, i.e. his own. And in some disreputable way this would be a matter for congratulation all round. I laughed when I recognized the stereotype, and wondered why it had taken me so long. I would know how to deal with the Colonel if he ever made the same mistake again.

Therefore I walked, in the muggy evenings, with the trees now dusty, the scent of petrol on the exhausted air, the streets enclosing me safely in their grids, their squares, their crescents; I passed on lightly in my landlocked freedom, my feet skimming the grey pavements, my hand occasionally stretching out to pluck a grimy leaf, my head quite free of reminiscence. Sometimes I covered miles in a single evening and returned home exhilarated rather than tired, rejoicing in the fact that I had found my old self intact, my wary enlightened self. The more I walked, the lighter I felt. I rarely saw the passing landscape. Most of the time I walked with head bent, hands in pockets, looking up only at occasional traffic lights, when I sensed rather than heard the bulk of an approaching bus, or when brought to a halt by a crowd of people emerging from a cinema. I liked these anonymous evenings and my feral wanderings: I liked to eat carelessly in Italian cafés with steam covering the windows, or drink coffee in the curious lounges of tourist hotels. Sometimes I would buy my supplies in those Asian shops which are the last to close, and in which the exhausted owner, his eyes ringed with darker brown, would extend a languid hand to remove my purchases from my wire basket: some washing-up liquid, a packet of tea, two grapefruit and a couple of foreign newspapers. I would postpone my return to the flat for as long as I could: only when I trudged up the many stairs would I realize how far I had walked. But my exertions always ensured a good night's sleep, without dreams of any kind.

It was a quiet summer. Eileen was on holiday in southern Turkey, so Robin and I manned the shop together. We got on extremely well, largely because neither of us spoke much to the other; our routines were so established, and we had known each other for so long, that there was not much need to speak. His odd appearance never bothered me, although customers often took him for some sort of caretaker. He dressed very formally in suits that looked as if they belonged to someone else and were vaguely crushed; I dare say he got them second-hand. In winter he tended to turn up in a raglan coat, rather short, and an old-fashioned soft hat. This summer he favoured a black cotton shirt and black trousers with pleats and pockets that stood out at the sides: standard wear in certain quarters in about 1952. Where he got this stuff I never asked, although I did sometimes speculate rather idly about his hair which was cut very short and from time to time appeared more irregularly auburn than at others. The collars of his defeated shirts were rather tight and the knots of his ties very small. He had, however, his occasions of splendour. For a night out at one of his clubs he would change into immaculate jeans and a polo shirt with a motif over the left breast, or a linen jacket, into the top pocket of which a pair of dark glasses would be inserted. I think it pleased him to dress like a poor clerk in the daytime and a man about town in the evenings. I sometimes wished that he would reverse the procedure, but he never did. I could quite see that after his evening swim he would want to change his personality; the working day would thus be symbolically washed away, and the real, the authentic Robin would emerge, as if after a baptism. I sometimes ran into him in the course of my evening walks, either coming home from the theatre or going off to one of his numerous clubs. As he lives just around the corner from me this was hardly surprising. Otherwise, our lives did not impinge. From time to time he would urge me to join him for a swim, but I knew how to deal with that one. He was never surprised and only mildly regretful; I think he had kindly ideas about companionship, of which I sensed that he had more need than I did. But he was very incurious, which I found restful. Perhaps that was why we got on so well; each of us was basically incurious about the other. We accepted each other, in a ruminative and casual manner, and moved like dreamers through our day, pausing occasionally for mugs of tea which he made in the back of the shop, and sometimes not speaking for hours.

In the evenings he seemed brisker and more purposeful. Once he asked me to join him for a drink and I idly agreed, thinking that we would go to the pub on the corner. He had in mind, however, a new wine bar that had just opened, an odd place, down some basement steps, specializing in elaborate cocktails, and staffed by men in mess jackets. Despite its restricted space it was got up to look like an ocean liner. There was even the standard well-dressed slightly drunk woman at the bar, trying to engage the barman in conversation, though I suspected that she too was on the staff.

'Do you come here often?' I asked, aware that this ritual remark was well in keeping with the spirit of the place.

'Only just opened,' he replied. 'Going to do well, though. Look over there.'

I saw a couple of well-known faces, or at least faces known to me from the gossip columns. I suppose this district is coming up in the world, although I cannot imagine how people can enjoy spending their evenings underground in this manner. I emerged thankfully into the hazy summer evening, breathing the dust-laden air. I left him there. I suppose that after keeping himself fit as he did he could stand the confinement better than I could. I preferred my odd hypnotic walks, and in his acquiescent way he accepted this. But it was kind of him. He often asked me to join him and never seemed to mind if I refused.

Days and evenings passed in this manner, and it occurred to me, with the sharpening of the weather, that I had not seen the Livingstones, nor made contact, for some time. I remembered my invitation to Heather and Michael, now rather diminished in urgency by the passage of time and my abortive telephone call, and I found myself somewhat reluctant to renew it. If, as I suspected, we had drifted apart, was there really any point in trying to drift together again? We had nothing in common, nothing really to talk about, and besides, I preferred my pared-down life to their awkward luxuriant alliance, with its attendant aura of unspoken explanations, their mutuality, which might conceal complicity or its very opposite. Heather had for me none of the charm of her parents, although I could see that she was programmed to turn into her mother; I somehow felt that this process would be less interesting than the finished effect of Dorrie's slightly anxious personality. Heather would be Dorrie with all the affection removed, repeating gestures which were, or had been, so attractive to me, but without their original grace. She would be either coarsened by her husband, or, in learning to ignore him, as she surely would,

85

retreat into mutism, a condition to which she was no stranger. In either case, she would fail to surprise me. I rather dreaded the evening I had promised them, but I remembered the look of pleasure with which it had been greeted, and I decided that I must make good that promise. It was only one evening to sacrifice, and after that it would be honourable to move into a more remote form of acquaintance. After that, surely, nothing more would be required of me.

Of course, I regretted losing contact with her parents, but that was perhaps also in the nature of things. Yet when I telephoned Heather's flat it was Dorrie who answered, and who sounded delighted to hear my voice. Heather and Michael were still in Spain, she said, and she and Oscar were looking after the flat for them. I expressed some surprise that they had been gone so long, but it appeared that Heather had been staying with them in Puerto Banus while Michael went off on his manoeuvres up and down the coast. He was obviously being encouraged to take on his father's responsibilities; as these were to me always mysterious, and as his father had remained in town – a matter to which neither of us would ever refer – I took it as a good sign, although it did seem to me a little odd that Heather should fail to accompany him. But they were both so much the children of their parents that perhaps it was not odd at all, or at least it was only odd to me. The marriage, as far as I could see, had not made much difference to any of them, or rather to their habits. This was perhaps what happened in bourgeois families, or just in families that kept a loving watch on each other. I have noticed that women who do well, have confidence in themselves, impose themselves tranquilly on the world, are precisely those women who have always been well looked after, have been prized, have represented to their parents their parents' best efforts. I did not doubt that even now Dorrie was carefully putting food into

Heather's larder, tidying her bedroom, arranging fresh flowers. She was one of those women who never arrive empty-handed, whose anxious loving care extends to everyone she knows. This great out-flowing of love had been accounted a sign of weakness, of immaturity, by her sharper sisters, who saw her set upon by thieves, spongers, confidence tricksters. But I do not believe that she ever was, thus confounding their expectations. It was they who brought to those tea-parties stories of exploitation by plumbers, shop assistants, traffic wardens, and who went through life in a cloud of suspicion. Dorrie herself was untroubled by all this, and by their forebodings. I suppose she had a charmed life.

'Rachel!' she said. 'How lovely to hear from you! Oscar and I were beginning to wonder what had become of you. Are you all right, dear?'

'I'm fine,' I said. 'I was wondering whether Heather and Michael might have an evening free to have dinner with me.'

'Well, of course, they'd love to, dear. We're expecting them home at the weekend. I'll ask Heather to telephone you. I know she'd love to see you again. What have you been doing with yourself?'

I told her that I had nothing to report, and then, aware that this might make me sound pitiable, enquired about their summer.

'Well, we've been in Spain, you know that, and we've had Heather with us, which has been lovely. I'm afraid we've been missing her terribly. Oscar has been quite down, although he would never admit it. And we haven't seen you either, which has been sad. We've been quite thrown back on each other. We've felt quite old. Well, we are old, I suppose.' She laughed sadly, as if almost unable to believe such a thing. I felt slightly impatient. There is no need to anticipate old age these days, and besides, she could not have been more than sixty. Oscar was perhaps a few years older. But living as they did, removed from the world's concerns, I supposed that they would notice little warnings, little alterations more readily. They were, in any event, so concentrated on each other's well-being that any tiny change of mood would be charted with alarm, even with genuine fear, for what could save either of them from the decline of the other? Perhaps they simply needed young company. I felt ashamed, then, of my long period of silence, and asked if I could come and see them. At this Dorrie cheered up immediately.

'Come now, dear, if you've nothing better to do. We shall be in all the evening. Come and share our meal. Oscar would love to see you. And we could tell you all the news.'

For news of Heather was sacred, and could not be delivered over the telephone. I arranged to go to Heather's flat after I had shut the shop.

I felt a renewal of affection for them, as I trudged along the Bayswater Road. Dorrie's simple greeting, her regret over my absence, were, after all, extremely heart-warming. And I wanted Oscar's advice, for Eileen was thinking of retiring and I wondered if I could afford to buy her share of the business. It would be a good thing for me to own half the shop: Robin and I could run it amicably together, although it would cut down on my free time. I often had thoughts of retiring myself, but of course that was impossible at my age. Nevertheless, it would be nice to be free. Freedom was not really a viable proposition, although an illusion of freedom – and it nearly always is an illusion – came to me in dreams, those same dreams in which I loved and drowned. What would I do with myself? After all, I was free now, I reflected; I had never been otherwise. Free to come and go as I pleased, free to walk the streets, free to find my own adventures. There was no lack of freedom in my life. On the other hand, it was very nice for once to be expected.

The evening was blue over the city, and the chill of autumn was in the air. In the park, cold seemed to rise from the ground; there was a smell of rotting leaves. I realized to my surprise that the year had turned. One always expects the summer to last for much longer than it does: one forgets the very sensation of being cold. Yet the people that I passed no longer had that expansive air that goes with the summer season; their heads were lowered, their walk purposeful. Shorter days and longer nights were upon us. I began to think about the trip I planned to Florence after Christmas, but for once I could summon little enthusiasm. I was beginning to find these journeys curiously purposeless, which to me was a bad sign. I had always managed so well, had returned to regale my friends with wonderful stories. Something amusing always seemed to happen to me. There was no reason why any of this should have changed. It was just the melancholy of an autumn evening, the symbolic dying of the light, that had affected me. The smells of autumn – chestnuts, chrysanthemums – were in fact rather tonic, the air crisp, reviving. I bought some flowers, their dense, heavy white heads smelling of pepper, and exhaling an irreducible coldness, and turned into the entrance of Heather's block of flats. After the night outside the faintly scented warmth breathed luxury and indolence. There was not a soul about.

Dorrie opened the door on to an even more exquisite smell, of something simmering in herbs and wine. She was flushed and pretty, and genuinely glad to see me. Oscar hovered behind her, his face creased into a smile.

'Oh, how lovely!' she said, burying her face in the flowers. 'You shouldn't, dear. But how sweet of you.'

'Dorrie,' I said. 'What is that marvellous smell?'

Her face became serious. 'I'm making a beef casserole for the freezer. You know how to do it, Rachel? Though I suppose you wouldn't want to make it just for yourself. But if you do, buy really good meat. And don't buy it in a supermarket. Go to a first-class butcher.'

'Dorrie, Dorrie,' laughed Oscar. 'Rachel doesn't want to hear all this. Come in and sit down, dear. We'll have a glass of sherry.'

They had clearly been lonely. That was my impression, as we all sat round the fire in the lavishly appointed room, which looked too big for the two of them. Curtains were pulled, lamps lit. As I drank my sherry, Dorrie continued her instructions, while Oscar looked on her with a loving eye. Once more I succumbed to their spell. I watched Dorrie as she continued with her recital of ingredients, then, launched into her subject, went on to detail even more splendid and complicated dishes. This soft little woman, with her tranquil expectations, her industrious use of plenty, seemed to me to be totally unspoiled by her good fortune. Her brows arched as finely above her large melancholy blue eyes as they always had done; her expensive silver-gilt curls still bore the mark of a department-store hairdresser rather than that of an elegant salon; she still wore only a wedding ring as adornment, and her blue pullover and skirt still bespoke a cautious attitude to fashion. But I noticed one thing that struck me with the faintest flicker of unease. She sat with her ankles crossed and her knees slightly apart, in that posture that old women adopt. It is a posture that defines lack of potency in an ageing woman, just as a broader stomach, the downward pull of gravity, defines lack of potency in an ageing man. It did occur to me then that her complaints that they had become an old couple were perhaps genuine. I began to see that they were already looking forward to the arrival of a grandchild to revive them. Until then, between the wedding and the christening, so to speak, they were in abeyance.

'I'm going to give you some to take home with you,'

she said. 'Just put it in the fridge and heat it up tomorrow evening.'

'You can also give her some of those biscuits you made,' Oscar added. 'You made enough to feed an army. They'll never finish them all.'

'When are they coming home?' I asked, for it seemed to me that their place was here. They had been away too long.

'On Saturday.' They spoke together, then laughed at each other.

'We had a lovely summer,' Dorrie said. 'She was with us for almost three weeks. But when she went to join Michael we found we missed her terribly. Silly, isn't it? After all, it's not as if we saw her every day before she was married. She worked very hard in the shop, and then she was away at the collections twice a year. But we always knew where she was, what she was doing. This time, when she left us, we didn't know where she was going, where she would be. And I didn't think she looked well.'

'Come now, darling, she was perfectly well. You worry too much. After all, she's a married woman now.'

'Yes, but she was so quiet,' said Dorrie, her forehead creasing into a frown.

'But Heather has always struck me as a quiet girl,' I put in. 'Calm. Quite a thoughtful person.'

This seemed to me as polite a way as possible of conveying Heather's mulish but amiable silences, her smile that gave the appearance of being remotely controlled. When I first met her I thought she must be deaf. When I got to know her better I revised my opinion slightly: I thought she was retarded. But when the evidence mounted up – the shop, her clothes, the way she drove her car, and the astonishing fact of her engagement and her marriage – it seemed to me that she was a creature of some depth, shrewd, as I have said,

91

but also possessing an admirable reticence, with the wit to know how to protect her inner life from the gaze of the curious. I appreciated this last trait: it is one I possess myself.

'And is she very happy?' I asked.

Oscar said nothing. Dorrie said, 'Yes, of course she is. I did ask her, and she said, "Don't worry, Mummy. Nothing has changed." Wasn't that nice of her? She wanted me to know that she was still our little girl.'

I looked at Oscar, whose face was expressionless. 'Some more sherry, Rachel?' he asked. 'Or would you like to eat?'

'It's only a cold supper, I'm afraid,' said Dorrie, recalled to order. 'A little consommé and a chicken salad. Or there's melon to start with, if you prefer it.'

We went through to an agreeably large dining room, with a round beechwood table and matching beech-wood chairs, and pale blue hessian on the walls. The food was delicious, of course, and my compliments were sincere. This encouraged Dorrie to regale me with more recipes and suggestions for dishes that I could prepare easily for myself. It was useless to tell her that I preferred to eat out: she would have looked at me in amazement. When we were seated round the fire again, and she had poured chocolates from a casket into various cut-glass dishes, and then darted up again to go and make the coffee, I asked Oscar about the shop. What would he advise? He smoothed down his tie, and told me that he would have to look over my books to see if I could afford it. If I would send him my bank statements for the past year he would go through them and see if I needed a bridging loan. He looked happier at the prospect of doing this. 'And what about the flat?' he asked. 'Have you bought that, yet?' I said that I calculated on being able to do that at the end of the year; it was to be my Christmas present to myself. 'Then, in due course, with the money you save on rent, you could

buy out your other partner,' he said. 'And you would
end up with a valuable property on your hands. And
eventually you could sell the lot and buy a small place
abroad. Enjoy a bit of leisure. You deserve it.'

'Oscar,' I said. 'Are you telling me to consult Colonel
Sandberg?'

He looked at me, I looked at him, and we both
laughed.

'Somehow, Rachel, that is something I would *not*
advise.'

We had a lovely evening. I succumbed once more to
Dorrie's warmth, to Oscar's kindness. I had to see the
wedding photographs, of course, which I did not think
a great success, although Dorrie and her sisters looked
lovely. But when I saw those two automata in their
white suits I felt as if I were being treated to excerpts
from a German ballet or opera, something by Kurt
Weill, perhaps. Even standing beside their wedding
cake they looked expressionless, with the same glassy
blue eyes, the same red lips. A blur in the background
was the Colonel, who had moved. Laughing at one of
his own jokes, no doubt. To go away in, Heather had
worn another suit, very narrow, in the rather hideous
pink that was so fashionable that year. It struck me that
she would not have been very comfortable sitting in that
skirt. It was Michael who was laughing in the final
photograph, his face subsumed into a double row of
childish-looking teeth. Sun flashed on the chrome of the
car, and on his tossed-back hair.

'These photographs are terrible, Dorrie,' said Oscar.
She looked disappointed but conceded that they were
not very good. 'The photographer was recommended
by Teddy Sandberg. No doubt he is better with villas
and time-share apartments. Things that don't move.'

'Oh, Oscar, don't be unkind. I think she looks
lovely.' Nothing would deflect Dorrie, who then produced from her bag more photographs of Heather at

various stages of her development. She had been a pretty girl, I saw, when she was young, and not yet withdrawn behind her remote smile. Even now she was rather striking. Between the *garçonne* haircut and the dangling jet ear-rings her face was quite classical, with a broad smooth brow and widely spaced eyes. But the face looked uninhabited and she had no change of expression. She looked, in these latest photographs, inanimate, not dead, but as though she had not yet come alive. I could not think of an appropriate comment to make. The impression was almost powerfully disconcerting.

'But look at the time!' I said. 'It's almost half-past eleven. I must have been keeping you out of bed all this time. Don't worry about me. I'll get a taxi.'

'You'll do nothing of the kind,' said Dorrie indignantly. 'Oscar will take you home. Oscar!' But he was already on his feet, searching for his keys. 'It's been so lovely to see you, Rachel. Don't leave it so long another time. We've missed you, dear. And we're always here if you need anything.'

I kissed her, and saw her standing at the door until the gates of the lift shut her off from my view.

In the car Oscar was silent. I said, 'Dorrie seems well.' He answered, 'She's well enough,' and then fell silent again. I felt a little awkward. When he stopped the car outside my shop, I turned to him and said, 'That was a lovely evening. Thank you so much. And I'll send you those papers, if you really don't mind. I would really appreciate your opinion.' He sighed, but did not move, and for a moment or two we sat there in silence. Then he sighed again, and turned round to face me. 'I don't like him, Rachel,' he said.

'Michael?' I ventured.

He nodded. 'I've tried to like him but I can't. There's something about him . . . He never looks me in the eye. He's never serious. Always laughing, joking. All about

94

nothing. And that father of his, always interfering. No, that's not fair. He doesn't interfere. He *advises*. And I don't trust his advice.'

'You don't have to take it,' I said.

He sighed again. 'If only the boy were less of a boy, there wouldn't be any need for all this advice. But he's not manly enough, Rachel. He never wants to stay at home. Always wants to go out in the evening. He says he's seeing clients but I think he just wants to go out and enjoy himself. I've noticed that he tends to sulk a bit. She lets him go, of course.'

'Heather is a wise woman,' I said. 'She's very shrewd.'

'She's too good for him.'

I laughed. 'You're bound to think that. They're only just married. Give them time to settle down.'

He sighed again. 'You may be right. But keep your eye on her. If she wants to talk to you . . . She wouldn't talk to her mother. She wouldn't want to hurt her. They've always been too close.'

I told him that I would telephone her the following week and he seemed resigned, after that assurance, to letting me go. But I got the feeling that he had more to say. It was only because I judged it unwise, at that stage, to let him unburden himself further that I moved to get out of the car. He would inevitably regret the fact that he had confided in me. I left him, with a further reference to my papers, and to the fact that I was in his debt. It was the only way I could think of to repair his self-esteem. I don't think he was taken in, though; the matter was too serious for that. I trudged up my stairs, with my box of biscuits and my jar of beef casserole, reflecting that my business with the Livingstones was not yet over.

95

S I X

As it turned out I did not telephone Heather the
following week because shortly after my evening
with her parents I succumbed to the prevailing bout of
flu and was extremely ill for about ten days. I lay in my
bed above the shop, waiting longingly for Eileen to
come upstairs and make me a cup of tea. I was not used
to being ill and the experience weakened me at some
fairly critical level: I was no longer the dandy of my
imaginings, invulnerable, amused, passing lightly
through life, with my feelings well protected. Over-
night I seemed to have come into contact with my own
mortality. Even when the fever had passed and I was
well enough to get up, I moved cautiously, testing my
movements, like an old woman, and frequently sat
down again in the middle of some fairly simple
sequence of actions, as if to ponder the necessity of
completing them.

Those days of recovery were some of the worst I can
remember. The routines of ordinary or real life seemed
to me quite meaningless. I remember spending obscure
and submissive afternoons in my small living-room,
conscious of the dust I was too weak to displace, feeling
subdued and sad as I contemplated the unlovely corners
of what had always seemed to me to be a perfectly
adequate flat. The iron smell of the over-efficient central
heating was in my nostrils as I sat all day, waiting for
darkness to fall so that I could prepare for bed. My
attitude to the dark at that time was amorous and
fearless: I was more than half in love with easeful death.
Recovery from this little illness filled me suddenly with
a distaste for my life. It was all unsatisfactory: my
home, my work, my 'prospects', for which I must

96

make such arduous arrangements. I felt a great need for some kind of recompense, one not earned by my own efforts; I had visions, entirely unwelcome, of that great good place that I could never reach. I felt a sourness within me when I contemplated my conduct. I knew that although it preserved me, it was not good.

In my weakness I was tearfully grateful for kindness. I looked forward to the moment when Robin's curiously unhealthy face would appear at the top of my stairs, after the day's work was finished, and I used to make up shopping lists for him, since he was kind enough to offer this service. The fact that I could not eat the food when he brought it was secondary; what I really wanted was to see a face, any face, at the end of those long unnatural days. I remember trying to eat one of Dorrie's biscuits and bursting into tears because I thought I must have looked so pathetic: I could see myself choking over this biscuit, as if it were a symbol of more beneficent days, and it was at this point that I realized that I must take some resolute action to bring myself back from this brink. I must become what I had always been, even though I did not like that person very much any more. But to risk this decline into heavy-heartedness was more than I could afford: I dared not remain in my weakened state. I therefore summoned the doctor, demanded vitamin injections, made a thorough nuisance of myself, recovered a little of my sharpness, and began to feel better. I began to eat again, and the descent into sleep was no longer quite so precipitous. After a few days I went downstairs to the shop, and although I made a shaky start I was soon my old self again.

Nevertheless, I felt weak for some days and excused myself from further effort. I had not left the building for over two weeks, and the weather, grey and somnolent, hardly tempted me to do so. With the tourists and visitors gone it seemed to me that there was a peculiar hush over the city; sometimes, when I stood in the

97

doorway to get a little air, I could hear the whine of a receding car die away in the distance before the next one caught up with it. We were not busy in the shop: it was the lull before the Christmas rush, and sometimes we sat all afternoon, reading, without being interrupted. Although I was used to this sort of daytime existence it did strike me as somewhat lacking in *joie de vivre*, but maybe I was still suffering from the after-effects of my illness, for I found it very difficult to invest my depleted energies in any activity whatsoever. Even making a cup of tea seemed to require a major decision. Finally, when the discomfort of my condition was too much for me to tolerate without a mild feeling of shame, I moved to the telephone to make my long postponed call. I could think of nothing worse than an evening at the theatre with Heather and Michael, but the irritation of not going through with it was almost as strong as the irritation of having to put up with it. Besides, they probably liked musicals. Already annoyed, I dialled Heather's number.

The voice that answered was toneless, which annoyed me even further. After all, I was the one who had been ill. Why couldn't she ever be the one to telephone? Why was I always expected to look after her? Why was her mind so apparently empty of the kind of thought that furnished everyone else's?

'Heather?' I said, in as enthusiastic a tone as I could muster. 'Hello. I'm sorry I haven't been in touch. I've had flu.'

'So have I.' The silence after this remark sounded final, as if Heather's flu had pre-empted any other kind.

Remembering how long it took to get her going, I made noises of sympathy, enquired after her regime, her temperature, her diet, all the while aware that similar enquiries were not coming in my direction. Made nervous by her monosyllabic replies, I enquired after Michael, after Dorrie, after Oscar: something stopped me from enquiring after the Colonel.

'What are you doing?' I asked, after another pause. 'Are you in bed?'

'No,' she said. 'I have to get up to feed the cat. Daddy bought me this little brown cat. I call her Phoebe.'

There seemed very little I could offer after this. 'Well,' I said. 'Let's hope we both feel better soon. I'll give you a ring in about a week's time, shall I? Maybe you'll feel like going out then.'

'It's very kind of you,' she said, again in that peculiar monotone. 'Actually, I don't think I shall feel like going out for some time. Perhaps you'd like to come round here.'

But Heather's flat was not the garden of earthly delights that Dorrie's house had been to me. If I thought of her at all it was with a slight feeling of oppression, for I seemed to see her marooned in that cruel blue bedroom, with the lustrous ice blue satin puff pulled up to her pale face. She had a marvellously white skin which never seemed to flush or alter: her recent fever, if anything, would have drained it still further. I felt a reluctant sympathy for her. I sensed that she would have been happier at home. It was about half an hour before I realized what a subversive thought this was, and yet it had come instinctively, unbidden. Heather *was* home; she was in her own home, even if it did look like something out of a colour supplement, put together from slightly outdated ideas of good taste. The royal blue towels and the French porcelain were in use, although I still saw them as piled up, inviolate, in untouched cupboards. Lives were actively lived in that flat, although in my mind's eye I saw it as empty of all activity, hollow and desolate. Heather's marriage seemed to have drained her of energy, exactly as if it had tired her in the way that Dorrie feared. In comparison with her present state, the Heather of the black garments, who had discoursed so enthusiastically of female

99

complaints, had been a positively dynamic creature, fuelled by her timid inclinations and her native watchfulness.

She should never have left home, I thought. Her marriage was an extravagance. Not all women are born to be married. Some exist quite happily in their original child-like state, apparently deaf to the demands of the body, or unable to interpret them, to pursue the path that leads to satisfaction. Not all women have the biological awareness to decode their impulses and to set out to find the partner who will give those impulses free rein. As far as I could see, Heather had failed on both counts, for in addition to her physical mutism, she could hardly suppose that Michael was a man to answer any unspoken need in her own life. No, she should never have married. She should have stayed with her parents, in that villa in the suburbs. She should have lived out her life in that bedroom that I had once seen, so different from the one she now occupied, a girl's bedroom, such as few girls have today, with flowery wallpaper and an apple tree just outside the window. Brilliantly clean, whereas I seemed to see that icy blue bedroom as through a haze, a mist of falling dust. I seemed to see the French windows standing open and a mournful wind scattering raindrops on to the carpet: I seemed to see curtains blowing and twisting, wrapping themselves round the legs of tables and chairs. In a curious sort of illumination I saw a pair of slippers, abandoned, one of them lying on its side. All of this, I thought, was the possible décor for Heather's recent illness. I felt also that the illness would confirm her ever increasing passivity.

I was therefore not much surprised to receive a call from Dorrie, urging me to go round and cheer Heather up. I explained that I had been ill myself, whereupon I received all the commiseration, all the sympathy that had been lacking so far.

'But you should have let me know, dear. I would have come round.'

I thanked her, reflecting that I had done quite well on my own, that further kindness would merely have encouraged me to languish. Heather, of course, would have been in receipt of all those encouragements to rest which anxious relatives visit on their cherished young. Yet she seemed none the better for them. I reflected on my own solitary struggle and tried to feel pleased with myself, but the effort had been too great: it had not only tired me, it had weakened me. And now that I was better I tried to put the whole thing out of my mind, as if it were an aberration best forgotten, something which I did not intend to share with anyone else.

When Dorrie urged me to go round and see Heather I assented a little wearily for I had not yet been out, and the Bayswater Road seemed to stretch endlessly before me, hedged around with incalculable hazards. It also occurred to me to wonder why Dorrie herself were not with Heather, although I supposed that Heather had something to do with this, that she had not wanted her mother to catch the illness, or that she had suddenly grown up and seen the irregularity of her mother's continued presence. Of Michael's part in her nurturing I thought it useless to enquire. He was the sort of man to hover nervously and jokily round the bedroom door before saying, 'Well, you don't want me hanging around,' and vanishing. No doubt he would come back later with ceremonious flowers and a bottle of wine, before changing his shirt and going out again. 'I'll leave you to rest,' he would say. 'Try and sleep. Don't worry about me. I'll have something to eat out.' And he would disappear, leaving Heather to her solitary contemplations, or whatever habitually occupied her inner horizon, and no doubt as lonely and bereft as I had felt myself to be, when I sat in my small sitting-room and wondered what had happened to me. And if he were to

101

catch the virus himself he would be terrified, not trusting anyone but his father to come near him. Again I felt that mingling of pity and distaste as I contemplated the vista of his childhood, the father's frantic and noisy ministrations, all lacking in conviction because of his overriding anxiety. And the anxiety passed from one to the other, like the parcel in that game that used to be played at the children's parties of my youth. And if the father ever got ill, catastrophe! I saw his habitually tanned face locked in discouragement, a thermometer sticking out of his mouth, the eyelids closed. And I imagined women of a certain age sailing up to his door, convinced that their hour had come, but unable to dislodge the whining pathetic little boy hanging round the foot of the bed. Poor Michael, destined always to be disliked by someone, possibly by everyone. There must be room for Michael in the universe, although it seemed that few people could find adequate reasons for his existence. Even Oscar, the kindest of men, had no use for him.

So I set out, on slightly uncertain legs, fuelled once more by the nervous exasperation that the thought of Heather's company always induced in me but reflecting that this visit would surely release me from the obligation of having to take them out, for the time being, at any rate. The walk tired me, and I was not encouraged to find Heather seated mournfully on her sofa, her expression blank, her hand mechanically caressing a neat narrow brown Burmese cat. Michael, who had opened the door to me, did not join us. Indeed, he disappeared immediately I had been shown into the drawing-room, only to reappear minutes later, to say, 'Well, I'll leave you two together. You won't want me butting in.'

Rather alarmed, as if I were to be held there in perpetuity until somebody else turned up to relieve me, I said, 'But I can't stay long. I must get back soon. This is the first time I've been out for nearly three weeks.'

'Nonsense.' This was accompanied by a knowing laugh and a wink.

'No, really, Michael. I've been ill myself.'

His face immediately became grave with exaggerated sympathy.

'I know, I know. But you look the picture of health now. And I'm sure you've got masses to talk about.' Again this illusion that we actually conversed. 'Make some tea, or something. Won't be late, Hetty.' This last remark was addressed to the back of the sofa.

'Are you in tonight?' Heather enquired, without turning round.

'Am I in? Of course I'm in.' He laughed uproariously. 'I'm just going down to the office to see if there's anyone I ought to meet. And if there is I'll get rid of them as soon as I can. Will you still be here, Rachel?'

I said I thought not.

'Well, give one of your friends a ring. Ring your parents if you're lonely.'

He was clearly itching to get away, and for once I couldn't blame him, for the atmosphere was clouded, and Heather expressed no desire for his company. Something had gone wrong, and this time I was inclined to blame Heather. Sitting there, with the cat on her lap, she looked bored and distant. I thought one should make more of an effort if one were married, even if one disliked one's husband, as she gave every appearance of now doing. I couldn't fault her for this, although it did seem to me that she had exhausted the possibilities of her new status rather rapidly. Surely she had always known what he was like? And even if she had only just found out, surely a little dissimulation was in order?

Heather sighed. 'Daddy said he might look in later.'

This he took as permission to depart. 'Well, I'll leave you to it.' He leaned over the back of the sofa as if to kiss her, but she averted her face, then immediately bent it to kiss the little cat. Michael laughed again; apparently nothing destroyed his irritating good humour. He flapped a hand at us both, abjured us to behave ourselves, and was gone. He was wearing a pale grey flannel suit, I remember, and a dark blue shirt, a combination which made him look as if he had just arrived from out of town. His face was still tanned and even a little flushed: he looked radiantly healthy. His consonants were as sibilant as ever, his gestures as emphatic, and were it not for the abundant fair hair I would have taken him for a foreigner, a Spaniard, perhaps, the loafer of the family, rich, infantile, well-heeled, not to be taken entirely seriously, happiest and most himself in places of light entertainment. Certainly he was out of his element in this high-ceilinged room, cold now in the receding light, the curtains shifting very slightly in the draught from a badly sealed window frame. The thought of him in that blue bedroom was one which I refused to contemplate, although I had certainly speculated about their intimacy the first time I had laid eyes on him. I had dismissed the idea then and I dismissed it now. He probably had a room of his own, I realized, that primrose yellow spare room that I had glimpsed when Heather had shown me round. Well, if that was the problem, they had surely come to terms with it. Again, I was inclined to blame Heather. Everything I knew about her contributed to this way of thinking. I had supposed that she had ruled this element out of her life as too obstructive, too likely to endanger her peculiar unstated decision to remain exactly as she was, too disruptive of her own settled and placid feelings. I had further assumed that she had chosen this partner precisely because with him she could not be changed into anything else and through him she would not be made vulnerable. I had even, remembering her shrewdness, thought it was a clever arrangement, a dispensation for her to enjoy the uninterrupted privacy

104

of her own mind. Although it was an arrangement which I thought ludicrous I could see in it evidence of advanced thinking. But now it seemed as if the system had broken down, although I did not see why it should, if that was what she had wanted. She probably had not reckoned on his being there all the time. With that I felt my old impatience with her rising to the surface. Some women avoid love – I do myself – because they fear its treachery. But such women, myself included, have to be pretty sure they understand their decision to do so. Heather, I could see, was quite simply unequal to the task of thinking the matter through.

Because I had thought it through myself I was inclined to disparage her attempt to do it the easy way. I had cut my losses early – no more sleepless nights for me, no more boredom either. I had made myself invulnerable and had found that I was free. But Heather, I saw, as I looked at her, still motionless, still mechanically stroking the little cat, had feared freedom, had sought the safer haven of marriage: marriage as protection, marriage as alibi, marriage as camouflage, marriage, in some odd way, as a continuation of her virgin life. And indeed there was no change in her expression to indicate that a disastrous mistake had been made. She was quieter, if anything, but who had ever known what she was thinking? Her expression was as blank as ever, her dark eyes as unblinking. She sat there, in unbecoming sage green, moodily, on the mediaeval sofa. She was beginning to wear the same colours as her mother, I reflected; in no time at all she would have graduated to printed silks. I wondered how I should tackle the question I felt should now be asked. Are you happy? Is everything all right? Were we at last to have the conversation that we had always avoided?

Nevertheless, I was inhibited from doing any of this by her lumpen immobility, her absorption in the cat, who now seemed to be her companion of choice, her indifference to what might be happening around her, and the fact that I had not been offered any tea. In fact I had not even been asked to sit down, but was left awkwardly stranded, as if my only purpose in coming had been to enquire after her health, like a delegate of a foreign power being received in audience. Michael too had been seen to stand and hover, although in his case reluctance to linger had kept him on his feet. As against this Heather seemed obstinately rooted, as if she would still be there when everybody else had been forced to leave. I thought I saw in this the power of possession – the flat was in her name, having been bought with Oscar's money – but this was out of character: she had always been unthinkingly generous, like her parents. But something in the set of her jaw and her brooding silence led me to think that whatever grievance had put her under this enchantment it was no mere material meanness. Nor was it the effect of her illness, for there was no perceptible change in her normal pallor.

'Heather,' I said. 'Are you all right? You don't seem quite yourself.'

She glanced at me briefly. 'Don't I?' she asked, unhelpfully.

'Perhaps being ill has tired you,' I said, rather annoyed by now. I was extremely mindful of the fact that I had been ill too. 'Or is something wrong?'

'Something wrong?' she echoed. 'What on earth could possibly be wrong?'

'Are you unhappy?' I said, exasperated by now. 'Are you disappointed? Are you bored? Are you having regrets?' My rising fury goaded me to ask these questions. 'Your mother appears to think you need cheering up.' No response. Exhausted, I dropped into a chair. 'Heather, is there anything at all you want to tell me? Anything you can't tell your mother?'

At last she turned on me that mild gaze that had been the despair of her aunts and cousins. I could see now, although I could not stop myself, that there might be something obscene about this goading of Heather, although she was so extremely unforthcoming that one was always tempted, and indeed felt entitled, to go too far. The gaze promised nothing but was held for a little longer than I felt to be comfortable. There did appear to be a speculative factor hidden somewhere within it but not near enough to the surface to be of any help. As my anger cooled I began to wonder if I had annoyed her, or at least unsettled her. But surely that was what I was there for, what I had always been there for. I tried again.

'Perhaps you're worried about something,' I ventured. Then a thought struck me. 'You're not expecting a baby, are you?'

At that she gave a single brief laugh.

'Well, it's not such an extraordinary idea,' I said, nettled again. 'Maybe you hadn't noticed because of the flu.'

'Oh, I'm sure I'd notice,' she said, with a touch of irony. She lifted the cat off her lap and brushed down her skirt. 'Don't worry, Rachel. You've asked all the right questions. You've done what my mother sent you to do. I'm perfectly all right. Let's have some tea, shall we?' And she got up and left the room.

There was no solving the mystery of Heather, if in fact there were any mystery at all. I looked round the room, which was cold, and felt a sense of dereliction. The grey light seeping through the windows made the green furnishings look sour. If it had been my room, instead of that small white bunker I called home, I should have lit all the lamps, put on the fire, pulled the curtains. As always, I appreciated luxury in other people without actively seeking it for myself. Mentally I changed the furnishings in that terrible bedroom – I could quite see that she would have no desire to languish there – and livened it up with patterns of red on the walls and more brilliant paint. If I had been Heather I

107

would have sat in the cheerful blue and white kitchen, furnished with all Dorrie's loving expertise, and made plans to go off to Spain with Michael. Even if he were unappetizing as a husband, he could still be, surely, a useful companion. And he would travel cheerfully, possessing that all-purpose good humour that would come in so useful away from home. I began to see that he might be unhappy too, having failed to secure from Heather the anxiety that had so protected him when lavished on him by his father. He would not register this as unhappiness, bearing as he did the hidden imprint of secret, private, unhappiness, the unhappiness of a child in a world populated by unreliable adults, but rather as discomfort, boredom, restlessness. There was no real harm in him. It was simply that he was untutored, that nobody read his mind in order to save him the trouble of trying to read it himself. But in a place where nature provided all the gifts – sun, wine, good manners, good humour – might he not gain more of an ascendancy than he could ever do here, in this important flat, with its too new furnishings, and the sinister light of an English November outside the windows?

There had been a touch of mockery in Heather's last remark which I considered uncharacteristic, at war with the euphoric image furnished by her mother. Poor Dorrie, who had always seen this marriage as a gift from an indulgent fate, had made her peace with it, had seen no change occurring in it, had thought it as well aspected as the material gifts she brought to it. Oscar, who had had reservations of his own, which he had heroically kept to himself, would be less surprised than even I was that the marriage had apparently already run its course, served its term. I seemed to see in this a partisanship which made me a little uneasy, for I felt that Heather's parents, blameless as they were, might be a little less indulgent to their daughter's inability to tolerate her husband, might have reproached her for her childishness, might have seen to it, in short, that she behaved herself. Her attitude to Michael had been one of fatigue verging on boredom, yet by now she should have seen that he required more of her, too much, perhaps, but not too much to incur that downcast expression, that concentration on the cat. What he required was protection, first and foremost, and then opportunities to amuse himself. As far as I could see, this was not enough to cause Heather to sulk. But of course she had always been the protected one, allowed to remain a child for as long as she wished, and then presented with a set of grown-up toys when the passage of time demanded them. I felt sorry for her, but I felt impatient too. It was impossible not to feel sorry for that creature on the sofa, blank-faced, as if she were in the waiting-room of a deserted railway station, as if the train for which she was waiting had already gone. Yet at the same time I wanted to shake her. Don't you know, I wanted to say, that many women would envy you, your home, and even your husband? After all, what is asked of you beyond a little tolerance? Michael may not be the world's most exciting man, but given the right opportunities I dare say he could make himself quite agreeable. I also saw that there was no point in my saying any of this, for someone as gently nurtured as Heather had been would not take kindly to my strictures, to any strictures. She would, on the contrary, look for sympathy, and no doubt receive it, from her parents most of all. I felt a spasm of distaste for her and for all those women like her, women who work for fun and marry for status, and still demand compensation. The only excuse for such women is incurable frivolity. And Heather was not even frivolous.

The sound of a key in the lock made me jump: Michael was back, and I did not want to confront him. But it was Oscar who came into the room, looking heavier than when I had last seen him. When he greeted me his eyes took on a watchful expression, the expression that used to be bent on Heather.

'Rachel, my dear,' he said. 'How nice of you to come.' He scooped up the little cat and began to stroke her, but his eyes never left my face. 'And what have you two girls been talking about?'

'Nothing, really,' I said. 'I think we're both too exhausted by being ill. Maybe we'll revive after a cup of tea. Heather's in the kitchen, seeing to it.'

I felt anxious in his presence, as if I had failed in my duty towards him. But he smiled kindly, seemed as if to relax, and lowered himself into a chair, with the cat on his knee. Sounds of spoons, being dropped, rather than lowered, into saucers, signalled a return to normality.

'Yes, it's a nasty business, this flu. You probably need a holiday. You didn't go away this summer, did you? You can always use our place in Spain, when we're not there, you know.'

'Perhaps Heather should go,' I said. 'But how would she manage at the shop?' How did she manage, I wondered, with all these honeymoons and other absences?

'Oh, didn't she tell you? She's found a manager, a nice chap. Calls himself Jean-Pierre, if you please. But otherwise perfectly sound. She's made him a partner. She's a limited company now – I saw to that. It leaves her quite free. And she trusts him absolutely. She'll just see to the buying now.'

'What a good idea,' I said. 'Then perhaps she should go to Spain. Catch the last of the sun.'

'Well, maybe she will. But she's going to Milan next week for the collections. Didn't she tell you? And I've persuaded her to have a few days in Venice afterwards. She has this Italian friend, Chiara. I thought it would be nice if they had a weekend at the Gritti.'

For of course life was easy if there was plenty of money, I reflected, and then felt a little ashamed of

110

myself, for I might have behaved in exactly the same way had my circumstances been different. But poor Michael didn't seem to be getting much of a look in. It amazed me the way that Heather and her father had closed ranks so easily. I detected in Oscar an unwise desire to detach his daughter from her husband which was a little too overt.

'And will Michael join them? The two girls, I mean.' I felt I had to say this, as if the poor fellow needed an advocate, as if plans were being made in his absence about which he knew nothing.

'Oh, I expect he has some business in Spain,' said Oscar absently, still driving a rhythmic and steady hand down the cat's spine. 'I expect they've both decided to be away at the same time. Ah, here she is. How are you feeling, dear?'

Heather's closed face relaxed slightly in her father's presence. She had assembled a tea of sorts, although the cake looked to be of Dorrie's make. They were really rather claustrophobic, I decided. But perhaps that is the curse of happy families, the curse of which they are unaware but which they visit on all outsiders. No doubt Heather would never get free of them, and might not even want to. As if in unwitting contrast, Oscar began to discuss my plans for buying my flat and then buying out Eileen Somers, which to me, although an obviously sound idea, represented a slow uphill slog of many years. I would need to take out a loan, and, as far as I could see, spend the rest of my life paying it back. But I liked the flat – at least I liked it when I didn't compare it with anything better – and I loved the shop. It was just that in moments of weakness, such as now, I wished that my life were not quite so reasonable.

With her father, Heather became once more the devoted daughter of the old days, quiet, amenable, acquiescent. Perhaps there was a more closed look about her, as there was about Oscar, but they seemed to find

111

contentment and security in each other's company. I almost expected Oscar to say, 'Where's your mother?' Where was she, in fact?

'How is Dorrie?' I asked, once again advocate for the absent.

'A little tired,' said Oscar. He put the cat down and took a cup of tea from Heather. That subject, too, appeared to be closed.

I took my leave of them as soon as I decently could. Their complicity disheartened me. I felt that Oscar was there in some protective or consolatory capacity which seemed to me faintly indecent. I had no experience of this kind of relationship, my own father having died when I was quite young, but I could not see myself behaving in the same way. I had always felt that adults should maintain a superior ignorance in this respect, and I felt Oscar to be too involved in Heather's domestic life, too watchful, too much a confidant. The very idea made me feel faint, as if the wretched Michael's secrets were laid bare. But he was essentially a man without secrets, too unwise to censor his very obvious childishness. Much as I disliked and pitied him, I disliked the idea of his being betrayed, in all his silly innocence, even more.

I found myself striding home, fuelled more by indignation than by returning strength, but recovering a little strength from the indignation itself. My supine acquiescence in all these stratagems, my enrolment as an additional protector, began to enrage me. With the clear light of prescience I realized that this situation could not be prolonged indefinitely, and that once I was out of sympathy I must either stay away or show my hand. In any event, I was fed up with Heather, who had tried my patience in her various manifestations for long enough. If she were not sufficiently mature to sustain her own marriage, she must see to it that the getting of wisdom must be her first priority.

The whole thing had been a waste of money, I thought, while simultaneously trying to calculate my own income and expenditure: Oscar had promised to look over my figures. These romantics with their elaborate weddings and their princely trousseaus, and not a thought, or not enough thought, for the sometimes sour and disappointed sensations that follow, as if the world is necessary to sustain the illusion, as if, left alone, no couple can wholly live up to it. This reflection served the useful function of reaffirming me in my independence, in my adventurous single state, in my disabused view of human affairs. I would press ahead with my own enlightened plans, I thought, and once I got home I would invite Robin for a drink and discuss with him the prospect of our partnership. As far as I could see, this would work perfectly: all it needed was a little planning, a little energy, a little goodwill. I turned to this prospect with relief after the insubstantial exchanges of the afternoon.

As it happened, Robin was just going off for his swim when I got back to the shop. He of course tried to persuade me to join him – he would never give up – but was easily diverted from this plan when I said that there was something I wanted to talk over with him, something to do with our future. Could he come back for a drink after his swim? Or would he like me to meet him somewhere? What about that peculiar wine bar he had once taken me to, the one with the lifebelts and the mess jackets? The Mauretania?

'The Titanic,' he said. 'Fine. See you there about seven.'

In the event I got there first and had to wait for him. I took a seat at the bar and ordered some fruit juice, then, thinking I looked a little too obvious, or rather, thinking I looked obvious when I had no plans for being obvious, I moved towards a table near the door. The place had filled up while I had had my back to it; sounds of laughter and a haze of smoke gave it an old-established air, although it was still fairly new. I rather lazily watched a knot of people who were evidently celebrating something or other, probably a business deal of some kind, as they were all men. A pearl grey flannel back evoked some vague reminiscence of something I had seen but it was not until the man wearing it turned round that I saw that it was Michael. He was in his usual state of hilarity, tossing back his leonine hair between each bout of laughter. He looked not in the least disconcerted at seeing me, but made no move to greet me. He did however move aside from the group he was with to raise his hand and give me his habitual wink. It was when he lowered his eyelid, in the glare of an overhead spotlight, that I saw that he was wearing blue eyeshadow. As he rejoined his friends, and burst into yet more laughter, I further saw that the glossiness of his lips and cheeks owed nothing to the suns of Spain, but had been obtained with instruments nearer to hand.

S E V E N

M Y first thought was that Dorrie must never know. The others, presumably, already did. Heather had found out, in her incurious way, and no doubt the secret was contained somewhere in that glacial bedroom; I had visions of Michael preparing for his nights out in the north light of those large windows, the pitiless and undifferentiated glare almost encouraging him to add colour to the scene. Heather would have told her father, no doubt trusting him to solve the problem, untie the knot, abolish the so inconvenient husband, who might or might not be a fraud. How did I know? I had never come across this little idiosyncrasy before. The Colonel had of course always known; hence the anxiety that was so striking a feature of his parental attitudes. His pre-marital behaviour now struck me as desperate, his relaxation at the wedding, and his sporting proposals made when Michael and Heather were away, as obscene. But Dorrie had no notion, I was quite sure. Dorrie still thought of her daughter as happily married, 'adjusting' to her new status, and perhaps a little 'tired' on account of it. Eccentricities of this sort could never figure in Dorrie's view of the world, where all was truly for the best, and patience was rewarded, and everything came to those who waited, and, naturally, the best was always worth waiting for. And so Dorrie must be protected, from her own incomprehension, as much as from anything else. I would say nothing, to any of them. The burden of this secret must be borne by each of us in isolation.

I left the wine bar without waiting for Robin: I would talk to him next day at the shop. I felt humbled and embarrassed as if the revelation affected me personally.

115

Out in the safety of the street I blushed when I remembered Michael's childish hilarity. It was the inconsequence of his behaviour that offended me: he had not appeared to mind that I had unmasked him but had gone on smiling and winking with as much fervour as if we were the best of friends. I began to wonder if he were in fact mad, or whether this were some super-refinement of the travel business, an attempt to persuade others of the beneficent results of living in the sun. Whatever the explanation he would have to go. I could see that. Even if Heather armed herself with the roughest of good humour, she could not be expected to tolerate a farce of this kind. There was something peculiarly menacing in the way the marriage had been engineered, as if the victim, in this case Heather, had been of no importance whatsoever; all that had mattered had been to provide a cover for this incorrigible child, so that he might enjoy his little games under the cloak of respectability. I wondered if I had missed any signs, if any of us had. But looking back, all I could see was that dreadful eagerness. And Dorrie had been as eager as the Colonel: I saw that now. In her desire to bring her daughter to that longed-for apotheosis, she had not minded too much that the bridegroom was of rather inferior quality. Dorrie was easily persuaded: her shopping expeditions proved that. And since she imputed all faults to herself ('I hope I did the right thing') she would no doubt quash any little misgiving she might have had before it even reached the level of consciousness.

And Oscar could not have known. Whatever instinctive objection he had had to Michael, whatever reluctance he had felt to the idea of Michael as a man, had surely been of a nebulous and general nature, for his own life had only prepared him for problems that were straightforward and in the nature of things, to be tackled with the patience and good humour that were

116

his professional attributes. Men like Oscar never discussed sex, let alone sexual peculiarities or aberrations; they would have felt a strong distaste at the very idea of these subjects being brought under the public gaze. In the days when we had gone to the theatre together I had learnt very quickly that he was only at ease with the noble passions. He was moved, I could see, by the idea of great and impossible love, the sort of love for which kingdoms were sacrificed, and which might prove to be fatal. Indeed, my strongest impression of those evenings we had spent at the opera was of the way that he and Dorrie had clasped hands tightly when such a love was heralded, as if in no circumstances could it be withstood, let alone rejected. They were curiously romantic for their age. For all Dorrie's joy in weddings, and the pride she took in Heather's engagement, it was true love which held her, which brought a look of mature recognition to her face, which convinced her of its inevitability, despite the warning signs.

I had been softened and amused by the solemnity with which they had accepted all the farrago of romantic passion. For to me it was a farrago, both on the stage and in real life, something archaic and unmanageable, unsettling and devastating, and to succumb to such a passion would be a quite voluntary step towards self-destruction. When I thought of those great operatic emotions I felt, for a moment, a quaking, a dissolution, as I had when I surrendered to the drowning waters of my dreams. I had no doubt that I would find the real thing as distasteful as I had that commotion, that violent and threatening disturbance that I had experienced when I consented for that one and only time to go with Robin to his health club, and immersed myself, as if fated to try to please him, in those blue and chemical waters. It was a mistake I would not make again.

I saw that I had no part to play in what must come next. If Heather had chosen not to speak to me, not to confide in me, there was no way that I could let her know that I had discovered her secret. I owed it to her pride to represent myself as passive and uninformed. And I did not see how I could be of any use to her unless I joined her in her dilemma. Truth to tell, I was as ignorant of what to do as she probably was herself: an annulment, I thought vaguely, should be arranged, but I had no doubt that the Colonel would put up a furious opposition to this. And Michael would of course be governed by what his father thought he should do. And there would inevitably be an unpleasantness surrounding this action, for many people would demand an explanation. I could see those sisters of Dorrie's retrieving the upper hand, sincerely shocked by the misfortune that had overtaken her but settling in quite comfortably to this new dispensation, which would return their little sister to them as innocent, and as in need of help and protection as she had always been. And did one return wedding presents in the case of an annulment, or were they just thrown in, as if the recipient probably needed or deserved some sort of consolation prize? I saw all sorts of indignity ahead. Yet the pretence could not be sustained. However impermeable Heather appeared to be, she could not be expected to put up with this outrage, this insult. I felt hugely angry on her behalf. Did the Sandberg ménage think her so stupid that she would not notice what was going on, or, worse, that she would not mind? I could think of no more gross behaviour to a woman than this indifference, this coarse bungling of her emotions. Whatever women put up with from men, they should never countenance indifference. Any violation of inner secrets is preferable. This was a surprising thought to me, for I usually err on the side of implacability, but for a moment or two I identified so completely with Heather and her gentle upbringing that it was I who had issued from that suburban villa, from that virginal bedroom with the apple tree outside the window; it was I who now sat in moral darkness in that pompous flat, with the wedding presents still inviolate in their cupboards, and only the little cat called Phoebe for company.

I no longer blamed Heather for confiding in her father. I felt for them both in what would inevitably be a sentiment of utter disarray, of helplessness, and, worse, of embarrassment. I could see that it was not good for a father and a daughter to meet on those terms, in such a situation, and that it might colour their relationship for some time, perhaps for ever. I could not think of a solvent for this situation. These things, after all, did not happen. To forfeit one's innocence in such circumstances was unimaginable. I could see further that Heather would not reclaim her innocence unless something utterly unexpected happened to her; if she stayed the same, she would stay tainted. My heart ached for her, as I thought of her trying to lead a normal life, to go to her shop, although there was little enough for her to do there now, with Jean-Pierre installed, or to sit out the time that she was condemned to spend with her husband. Significantly, the Colonel had begun to make himself scarce: I could picture him tiptoeing like a marauder from the scene. No doubt he would return if he sensed that trouble was about to be made. By 'trouble' he would understand any righting of the wrong in which he had been instrumental. And Michael would of course profess smiling ignorance of what the trouble might be. One of the main difficulties of talking to Michael had always been to try to get him to be serious. He spoke in clichés, and no doubt some psychic trick had taught him to think in clichés. They would get no help from Michael, who would maintain his unfocussed *bonhomie* until such time as events really threatened him with exposure or, more probably, dispossession, when he would instantly break down into hysterical panic. Trying to deal with him in that condition would be even worse than trying to breach his habitual radiant indifference. And yet I still felt a twinge of pity for him and his terrible life. I could see his frightened face, as in fact I had never seen it, or had seen it only in that misty anteroom in which all these sightings of mine took place. And I could see him back with the Colonel, cramping his style again, and the Colonel's lady friends not too pleased about it. Everyone would lose face. It was not to be borne. But the only alternative was to go on as if nothing had happened. That was not to be borne either. There was no way out.

I remember that the weather deteriorated sharply at about this time, as if in sympathy. I awoke every morning to the sound of water gurgling through a broken pipe into a drain blocked with leaves; the sound of that steady surreptitious progress, the thought of the puddle that would inevitably form and into which I would be forced to put my hand, produced all the usual shudders in me. Finally, when it looked as if my little courtyard would flood, I had to ask Robin to do it. All day we sat with the lights on as a grey mist of fine rain blurred the street outside. Customers were few, and those who did come made a mess with their dripping umbrellas. We were constantly mopping the floor, and trying to protect the stock from wet hands and elbows. I was exasperated by all this water which prevented me from going out or feeling well; my eyelids seemed to thicken and my vision to blur, my legs to stiffen and my ankles to swell, as if I were really the victim of a physical affliction, an allergy to the dripping skies which rendered me inactive, incompetent, ineffective. I chose to look on the weather as an element which would put a stop to all social movements; I chose to think of everyone as immobile as myself. In this way I managed to still my conscience over my silence. I knew that my sympathy for Heather should have prompted me to take

120

some action, to proffer some sort of invitation, even if it was refused as mournfully as I expected, but I could think of no way in which I could be helpful to her if the truth lay unexamined between us; I lacked the patience to let her fears subside in my presence. I was always slightly rough with her, as if I could galvanize her in this way, but it was never a success. I lacked gentleness, I supposed; perhaps she was right not to trust me. I felt wretched when I faced up to this truth. I felt as if I had accepted friendship on false pretences. And yet I was not sure that Heather had ever really accepted me as a friend. In some ways I was almost sure that she disliked me. I think she disapproved of me, thought me shallow, too pleased with myself. Although I had never confided in her I rather fancy she knew quite a lot about me, and what she knew did not amuse her. Heather was shrewd, and she kept her own counsel. In many ways she would have made a very responsible adult if fate had allowed her to be one. I knew that I would have to make some sort of gesture sooner or later, if only to relieve my own anxiety and sore feelings on her behalf, but I kept putting it off until the weather improved; this veil of water prevented me from thinking clearly, deprived me of initiative. I was always glad when night fell, releasing me from any obligation to initiate action. I was hardly going to invite them to the theatre now.

The weather put a stop to all my activities. Every evening I got into bed earlier and earlier. It was as if I were travelling backwards, back into childhood. I slept voraciously and was aware of dreaming copiously, although I always forgot my dreams as soon as I awoke. In any event, these dreams were of no consequence to me or of interest to anyone else. Down this dwindling corridor of reminiscence, as if some shreds of the night were slow to leave me, I saw the two white-clad figures of Heather and Michael dancing at their wedding, I saw Oscar starting up with a cry of alarm, I saw the Colonel

121

laughing with relief. Whatever I saw I did not like. And all this was involuntary, the product of those unconscious hours when I was not aware that I was seeing anything at all. The mornings found me irritable, unsettled. I put off speaking to Robin about the partnership, dithered about completing the purchase of the flat. All that was required of me was a little decisiveness, and yet some kind of sick caution held me back. For a time I was afraid of making any kind of movement. I suppose that I was generally confused about initiating any kind of action. I knew what I should do, in many directions, and yet I could not get myself to do any of it.

One afternoon, as we were sitting listlessly in the shop, and Eileen had gone off to do her Christmas shopping, I realized that if trade did not pick up we were going to have a disastrous year. This frightened me, and I recovered a little of my boldness. I asked Robin if he could spare me a moment, and I asked him what he thought of the prospect of having me as a partner. His face brightened, and he said that he assumed that that was what I had always had in mind. I explained that the flat was my first priority, and that I might have to keep him waiting until my affairs had settled down and I could put matters on a regular basis. In fact, that I might have to borrow money from him in order to buy Eileen's share of the business, and although I expected to pay interest on the loan he might have to wait some time before we were on a proper business footing. He appeared to raise no objection to this, although I felt as if I might be taking advantage of him. I don't know why I felt this: Oscar had advised me to speak to the bank, but I hated the idea of having to ask the bank for another loan, and I trusted Robin, who had no inconvenient plans for improving his life away from me. In fact he gave in so easily that I insisted on our having a regular arrangement and a formal agreement; some sort of document would have to be drawn up, some sort of

122

calculation made that would leave him feeling happy and leave me feeling a little less adventurous. I could see that this might lead me back to Oscar, a direction I did not particularly want to take, and so I delayed this too, and in doing so merely increased my feeling of unease and of insecurity.

My attitude towards the flat also underwent a slight change at this time. Surveying it when I went upstairs in the evenings brought no sense of comfort or relief. I began to resent its blank white walls, its curved metal windows. The heating, which I kept on full, in an attempt to defeat the pervading damp, made the air smell dusty and tightened the skin on my face; I began to see that little concrete warren as unlovely, although it had always seemed perfectly satisfactory to me before. I had a vision of myself growing old in that white sitting-room, and I did not like it. Of course, I could refurbish it, make it look a little bit more welcoming, although I was bereft of ideas for making it more lovable. It had always seemed to me quite adequate, mainly because it left me alone, stretched out no feelers of affection or fondness that would retain me there. It was, I saw, a flat to get out of rather than one to stay in. It was a machine for eating and sleeping in, a suitable dwelling for a working woman, whose main interest is in her work. I disliked this version of myself, which seemed to negate my other activities, reduced them to after-hours amusements, whereas I had always thought them pretty central. These mute white walls had been silent witnesses to many encounters; nevertheless, they withheld comment, and their very withholding struck me as unfriendly. '*Unheimlich*' was the word which came to mind when I stood on the threshhold of my bedroom: I had read it in some psychiatric textbook which I had picked up one day in the shop. 'Unhomely' was too mild a translation to convey the effect of alienation that the German original possessed. In a half-hearted way I began to wonder if the effect might be different if I pulled the bed nearer to the window instead of leaving it stranded in the middle of the room. Then I realized that this would involve moving everything else, and that in order to do this I would have to enlist Robin's help yet again. Something prevented me from asking him for this perfectly reasonable help: I felt faint-hearted about everything, and in the end I left the room exactly as it was.

With a supreme effort of will I telephoned my landlord and told him that I was ready to purchase, and that if he cared to call in some time during the following week I would be very happy to sign the agreement and hand him the cheque. Having done this, I retreated upstairs again and looked blankly at the flat, as if in wonder that it had ever meant anything to me. The idea of staying here for the rest of my life appalled me. It was while I was contemplating this prospect that I heard Robin's feet on the stairs, and, turning my head, saw his face through the door which I had left open.

'Nice, isn't it?' he said. 'Although you could do with a different colour on the walls.'

We looked at the sitting-room, which seemed to be awash with the weeping light of the rain spattering the windows, and could think of no improvement that would make it look either bigger or better. I remembered those terrible days of convalescence, in which I had sat here unmoving, unthinking, remembering my dead parents, and almost unconsciously assuming the pitiful position that my mother had assumed in her last days. The thought filled me with horror now as it had then; in fact all my thoughts were veering towards sadness. I blamed the weather again, unwilling as I was to concede to a general feeling of desolation.

'Buy a few engravings,' Robin was saying. 'Or posters, if you're a bit short. By the way, there's someone downstairs asking for you. A Mrs Livingstone. No one we know. Doesn't look like a customer.'

Dorrie! I flew down the stairs, ridiculously grateful for the interruption. Even if she had somehow come to ask my advice about Heather, advice which I was quite unprepared to give, my spirits lightened at the thought of seeing her without in some way having engineered the meeting. I found her standing in the middle of the shop, looking around with interest and a little awe. She was wearing a smart black satin raincoat, which was stained with damp across the shoulders, and a headscarf printed with a design of horses' bridles. She had a number of parcels and a dripping umbrella in her hand. There was some undefinable loss of chic in her appearance, which I put down again to the weather. Who could look chic in this rain?

'Rachel, dear,' she said, her face brightening, as I went forward to embrace her. 'I hope you don't mind my calling in like this. I met the girls for lunch, and then I went to the flat to leave one or two things, and I was on my way home, and I thought I'd stop off and see you. It's been such a long time. And I dare say you don't want to come and see us now that Heather's no longer at home. We wondered how you were.'

'But Dorrie,' I said. 'You know I always love to see you. And I was going to telephone Oscar about some business he was kind enough to advise me on.'

'That's all right then,' she laughed. 'And this is where you work? It's lovely, Rachel. You have done well, dear.'

'You must come upstairs and have some tea,' I said firmly, 'and take off those wet things. I'll put the kettle on. Just follow me up.'

'I was hoping you would say that,' she confessed. And, apologetically, 'I brought a few cakes.' She handed over a white cardboard box. 'I hope I did the right thing.'

'Rachel,' she whispered, behind me on the stairs.

'That young man looks very nice. He was charming to me. Is that your partner?'

'Yes,' I said. 'That's Robin. We get on very well.'

'I'm so happy for you, dear.'

'Oh, Dorrie,' I laughed. 'We're business partners, nothing else. We've known each other for years. In fact, our fathers knew each other, on paper, at least. Both our fathers were booksellers, you know.'

'I expect they'd be very proud of you,' she said. 'And this is where you live? It's very pretty, dear. So nice and light.'

I switched on as many lights as I possessed, and, although it was very warm, the fire as well. I did not see how she could possibly like this room, so different from her own. But she told me that when she and Oscar were first married they had lived in just such a little flat, and had only gradually saved up to buy the house in Wimbledon. All the additions had come later. And she told me that they had been very happy in their white flat, that it did her good to see something so like it. She did so hope that I would be as happy as they had been. Seeing the flat was, she thought, an omen. She was sure I was going to be happy.

Knowing the direction of Dorrie's thoughts I said nothing, but helped her to remove her raincoat, which I took into the kitchen to dry. She kept her headscarf on, saying, 'No, dear, my hair's such a mess.' I opened the box of cakes and put them on the prettiest dish I could find; then, with the tea in front of us, I began to like my flat rather better, to see it in a kindlier light.

The cakes were predictably delicious, but I noticed that Dorrie's fork merely broke hers up and played with the pieces. She drank her tea thankfully, but her lips trembled slightly. I looked at her. Surely Oscar could not have told her what I already knew? Surely he could not have found the words to enlighten her?

'Dorrie,' I said, carefully. 'Is anything wrong?'

126

She started slightly, then abandoned her fork, and pushed her plate away.

'Why, no, dear,' she said. 'I expect I just miss Heather a bit. She's in Milan, you know, at the collections. And then Oscar said something about her having a weekend in Venice with her friend Chiara. Chiara lives in Venice, or comes from Venice: I don't exactly know which. Oscar is treating them both to a weekend at the Gritti. They will both be so tired. I think it's a lovely idea.' But her hand trembled slightly and she put down her cup.

'The fact is,' she went on, 'I'm quite glad to know that she's away. I'm going to get myself tidied up, while she's taking a break. Just a couple of days in the Clinic. And it will all be over by the time she gets back.'

I felt cold. 'Why, what's wrong?' I asked, in as lively a tone as I could manage.

'Just this silly little lump.' She untied the headscarf and proffered an inflamed earlobe. 'I'm sure it's nothing. But Oscar fusses so. And it's no good to me where it is, is it? So Oscar insisted on the London Clinic and I go in tomorrow afternoon.'

She sat back and laughed a little shakily.

'And you're not telling Heather?' I asked.

'Well, no, there's no need to worry her. She's been a little nervous lately. And truth to tell, Rachel, I wondered whether there might not be a baby on the way.' She laughed again, this time with pleasure. 'Of course, that would make us all very happy. The Colonel too, I'm sure.' She lowered her eyelids and tried to eat a fragment of cake, but failed. 'You won't tell her I told you, will you, Rachel? She hasn't discussed anything with me yet. Oscar says I'm romancing, but I think I'm right.'

I struggled to disguise the horror I felt and I must have succeeded, for she said, 'I can see you're not surprised. I think she'll make a good mother, don't you, Rachel? And Michael will be such fun as a father. I sometimes think he's such a boy himself. But I mustn't keep you.' She retied the headscarf. I could think of nothing to say.

'I'll come and see you, shall I?' My voice sounded strange to me, but evidently perfectly all right to Dorrie.

'Well, there's no need, of course, dear. But it would be lovely. You know, we think of you as almost a daughter. And you're so sensible. I'm sure Heather's lucky to have you as a friend.'

When she left, after many protestations that I was not to put myself out, that it had been lovely to see me and my flat, and that she was so glad that everything was going so well for me, I sat down heavily. I must have sat for some time, in the darkening room, for I had instinctively turned off the lights after she had left; the next thing I knew was a knock on the door, which was Robin, come to tell me that he was locking up.

'Nice woman, that,' he said. 'You okay? You look a bit pale.'

I said that I was fine, and that he should come in late the following day: I would take care of things in the morning, but I might be gone in the afternoon. Eileen's presence tended to be fitful, when she had gifts for her family to buy. Neither Robin nor I had any family to speak of, although he had once mentioned a married sister in Shropshire, with whom he did not get on too well. There was no problem about our attendance.

I spent a terrible evening. My mind veered away from the Livingstones and their problems, although I knew that those problems would reclaim me, would require my most urgent consideration, once I came out of this peculiar trance that had overtaken me. For a time I paced round the room, coming to rest occasionally at the window, my hands patting the too-hot radiator, staring drearily out at the fuzzed haloes of the street lamps. Thinking I might feel differently once I had shed

128

my daytime persona, I went into my bedroom and changed my clothes. Then, haplessly, I drifted back into the sitting-room, and sat down in my usual chair. I was not hungry, which was just as well, as I had forgotten to buy any food. I picked up a book from the pile on the table at my elbow, and read, 'Lacking more serious occupations since 1814, I write, as one might smoke a cigar after dinner, in order to pass the time.' I put the book down again, disheartened by this dandyish attitude, so impossibly urbane as to be permanently beyond my reach. The empty evening disturbed me, and I wished that I had urged Robin to keep me company: I could always have scrambled some eggs. My life seemed to me to be insubstantial, my company and presence marginal. In the morning, I knew, I would have to face up to being all these things, to hold myself in readiness as a good friend, as a support, as a comforter, an utterer of sturdy and bracing clichés. I would have to substitute myself for the absent Heather, but only in such a way as not to usurp her importance, her uniqueness. And then, when poor Heather came back from her unrealistic holiday, I would have to indicate to her that she must lay aside her own burden for the time being and allay her mother's fears, while at the same time disabusing her mother of any fond fantasy that might be present in her mind. And, whether I liked it or not, I would have to engage Oscar in some close business discussion, to do with my growing involvement with my little shop. Suddenly I wished it were all mine, that both Eileen and Robin were gone, and that in the complete silence left to me I might remain undisturbed. And then, I thought, one day, when they had all returned to their proper preoccupations, I would make my decision, pack my bags, hang a sign saying CLOSED on the door, and simply disappear. I would not be missed. Dorrie might say, 'What's become of Rachel? We never hear from her

129

these days,' but in time even she would no longer ask. I knew what had put me into this state of mind. The spectacle of illness, with its attendant train of cheerfulness and dread, had laid its chill hand on me. I rehearsed it all: the packing of presumptuous nightgowns into the suitcase, as if those fine materials might remain unsullied by the blood and waste that would certainly issue; the final appointment with the hairdresser, so as to put a good face on things; the arrangement of meals, to be heated through and eaten on a corner of the kitchen table by the one who would leave the dishes, and maybe the food as well, in his haste to return to the hospital; the enormous courage needed to make all those obligatory jokes; the trembling moment when the visitors left, and one was reduced to reading the Get Well cards; the secret descent into fears that must never be shared. I had lived through all this once, and although it seemed ridiculous to transfer this burden of associations to a woman who was merely going to have a small cosmetic operation, I knew that I would not have too easy a time for the next few days. For a moment or two, I felt a return of my old exasperation when I thought of Heather swanning it at the Gritti Palace: why did she have to be spared this ordeal, when she was the obvious person to bear it? My old weariness at the thought of Heather as a protected species, whose feelings, whose very ignorance, had to be safeguarded, gave me back a little of the energy I seemed to have lost throughout the long hours of this day that would not end. Then I reminded myself that Heather's own ordeal had only just begun, and that it was of such a singular nature that she could not be expected to bear it alone, and that all her champions must be in good order if she were to succeed.

Above all, I felt a regrettable cynicism. These people, with all their hardships, were so fortunate! Even these hardships came into a special category: a few adjust-

130

ments to be made, and they would be back on course, with no grievous loss sustained, no vital organ impaired. And suitable arrangements would be made for their protection throughout, holidays scheduled for their recovery. A place in the sun would be waiting. Without a realistic attitude to what was happening to them, sympathy would always be misplaced. The curse of happy families again, looking excitedly after their own, making the outsider feel benighted. But the additional curse of happy families, I reflected, was to fear the loss of one of its members, to be unmanned by every accident that could befall a child or a husband or a mother. The lives of the happily united were not necessarily tranquil. In fact everything was precarious: those who live in solitude need only fear their own mortality.

And I seemed, once more, to be feeling mine. The shadow of illness darkened my little room, brought to mind all the illnesses I had endured, and, so far, survived, dredged up from the past memories which I had suppressed but which had remained intact and were waiting once more to claim me. The deaths of mothers, of fathers, expunged from my consciousness, made me once more start up in horror. I rushed to the bedroom again, opened my wardrobe, instinctively chose a plain but flattering sweater and skirt, made up my face, prepared to go out. It is something I have to do from time to time. I have my own techniques for dealing with such sieges and fugues as lie in wait for me. I assume that rough good humour that I once prescribed for poor Heather, I force the note. I go out, seek companions, bear them home. I live on the surface, plunging ahead, attached only to the present, with only a wary eye to the future. No bourgeois sentiments for me, no noble passions. The surface, the surface only.

It was just that somewhere in my mind – for the mind contains everything, the past, as well as all the people

131

one has ever been – I still retained the affections of childhood, and with these affections I encompassed the Livingstones. It was somehow possible for me to feel for them all the trust, all the love, if that is not too sentimental a word, that I had once felt and that may have got lost somewhere along the route I had since travelled. I would play my part. With them I would always play my part. But in order to play my part I might have to create my own form of sustenance. As I pulled the belt of my trench coat tightly around my waist I looked round once more at my little room. It seemed meek, abashed, innocent, as empty rooms with their lights on often do. Although created without love, the room remained my witness. The coffee cup on the table, the Stendhal, still half open, on the arm of the chair, had their own incorruptible life and seemed to reproach me with their gravity. But I had had enough of gravity for one day. The supreme irony, to me, was that in the Livingstones' little drama I was the one cast as the wise virgin. I laughed, switched off the lights, and went out into the night.

E I G H T

THAT night I slept like a stone. When I awoke I sensed that the rains and mists of previous days had disappeared, to be replaced by the first frosts of winter. It was the end of November: our busy time was just beginning. There would be four weeks of frantic activity followed by flat calm after the New Year when everybody spent their money at the sales. This was when I usually went away, although this year I was going to be too much out of pocket to manage it. I had a little emergency money put by for such occasions, but at the moment I was unwilling to risk spending it: if things went smoothly, and we had a good Christmas, I would go away at Easter. Some caution, and not only over the money, warned me to be on hand, in case I were needed. Or maybe I was getting tired of my way of travelling. I found myself unwilling to take up the burden of providing my friends with amusing anecdotes, largely, I must confess, to persuade them that I was still, as it were, in credit. My friends were rather of the competitive variety, spreading an aura of successful propaganda around their every activity. I suppose most women are like this; at least most of the women I know seem to be. At the heart of their energetic performances – and such women are not always soothing to be with – lies the desire to persuade others of their great talents in the game of love, their allure, their knowledge, their expertise. Stunning ripostes are theirs, famous scenes are staged, advances are scorned or rejected, new lovers assumed as of right. Circe-like, such women turn men into swine. I do it myself: it is the best protection. It is also rather boring, but the only alternative seems to be something incredibly demanding, for which I am un-

133

prepared and for which in any case I do not have the time. And of course yet another alternative is the fate undergone by poor Heather, a pompous and futile marriage, no love, and a lot of embarrassment.

In spite of her current fiasco, Heather had a sort of obstinate decency, I thought. She had never offended anyone, to my knowledge, nor was she likely to. Certainly she had never offended me, never scored points, never dropped hints or made indelicate enquiries. Such discretion is rare in a woman, certainly among the women I knew and who counted as my friends. Throughout the weeks preceding Heather's marriage, when gifts and acquisitions seemed to be raining down on her from heaven, she had never shown off. Dancing industriously at her own wedding, she had noted my arrival, waved her hand, pointed to a table, and mimicked that she would join me later, when the music stopped. I thought that was very nice of her, considering that we had never had anything in common, nor could we be said to be friends in any real sense of the word. Caution seemed to be her watchword, although it had let her down pretty badly, and her mildness of manner precluded any act of aggression on her part. It was only that it was difficult to get very interested in her, just as it seemed difficult for her to get interested in anyone else. Yet in the long run I did not doubt that she possessed some kind of strength. How this would manifest itself I did not know, but no doubt occasions would arise: they always do. Maybe her absence at this time was a sign of strength, although I thought that she should have picked up enough hints from her mother to put off this particular visit Milan, and certainly her weekend in Venice. Even in this I saw something of that fixity of purpose that led me to suppose that she had her own best interests at heart.

When I reached the London Clinic shortly after six that evening it was to find Dorrie in bed, in a prim white nightgown, and her two sisters seated accusingly at her side. Faith in the powers of doctors ran high in that family, and the general feeling seemed to be that Dorrie should have had regular check-ups in order to ascertain that she was all right. Her current malaise, they seemed to assert, was entirely her own fault. She had brought it on herself with the fatigue of the wedding preparations and the constant provisioning of Heather's flat. When she protested that she felt perfectly well they made scornful and exasperated noises. Certainly she looked well enough to me, although she did have the victimized look of anyone seen in bed when others are fully dressed and going about their normal business. She was in a small room, already well furnished with flowers and baskets of fruit. All the lights were on, which seemed to me fatiguing, as did the conversation. Dorrie was called upon to answer many questions, and to allay many fears. The anxiety of Janet and Rosemary, discharged with magnificent lack of tact, brought forth all her powers of submission. She assured them, as they should have been assuring her, that it was only a matter of a few days' rest, and then the tiny operation: of course they had to do certain tests, she said, but that was simply a matter of routine. And the rest would certainly do her good. On this, fortunately, they seemed to agree. They were also firm believers in the efficacy of rest, would lie supine every afternoon, before getting up with a sigh and agitating themselves with renewed vigour. I judged this as good a moment as any to make my presence known.

'Rachel,' said Dorrie delightedly. 'How lovely of you to come. You remember the girls, don't you?'

The girls seemed equally appreciative, and murmured with pleasure, getting up and rearranging the chairs round the bed. That was what so endeared them all to me: their lovely welcome. I bent down to kiss her, and smelled her honeysuckle scent, mingled with clean bedclothes. She had made up her face carefully, I noted; the girls, too, were dressed ambitiously, as if to outweigh the terrors they too obviously felt. I seemed to be the only one present prepared to take this little episode philosophically, although I did wish that Heather were present, if only to free me for more pressing duties at the shop. It looked as if I would have to stand in for her until such time as she chose to return. Again I felt something of the old exasperation, although this was clearly not the moment to entertain any feelings of my own. In any event it seemed to be generally acknowledged that my stolidity, my stoicism, if you like, and my position, far removed from their more intimate concerns, would stand them in good stead, were precisely what was needed in the atmosphere of hospitals, particularly as the atmosphere was, in the present case, so nervously enjoyed. A place was found for me between the two sisters, and, as I laid my little bunch of anemones on the counterpane, they exclaimed once again at my thoughtfulness, my appropriateness. I think that they were relieved to have me there.

'Well, Dorrie,' I said, as carelessly as possible. 'When do they attend to your ear? You will look like Van Gogh, you know. You had better take up painting.'

'She used to do lovely watercolours before she was married,' said Janet. 'Such a pity to let that talent go to waste.'

'Oh, once I was married I had more important things to do,' laughed Dorrie. 'And I was never all that good. I used to paint flowers,' she told me. 'Mother had a rose garden, and I tried to paint them all.'

'I've still got two.' This was Rosemary, her face softened in reminiscence. 'They're in Sarah's old room. Wasted in there, now that I come to think of it. Nobody uses it now. But they look so pretty, on either side of the window. I've got Mother's tallboy in there too. I think I'll take the bed out and make it into a little

136

sitting-room. What do you think, Dorrie? I don't know why I haven't done it before. After all, she's not likely to come home again, is she?'

A general sadness over the departure of daughters seemed likely to invade the little room. I hastily picked up the menu which was lying on the bedside table.

'Duck à l'orange,' I mused wonderingly. 'Sole Parisienne. Does anybody eat all this?'

'Oh, yes, dear,' said Rosemary, with authority. 'People with broken legs.'

'What have you ordered?' I asked Dorrie.

She closed her eyes momentarily, as if faint at the thought of food. 'Vegetable soup,' she said. 'And an omelette. I thought something light for this evening.'

It was at that moment that the thought occurred to me that she might be really ill. That Dorrie should feel repugnance at the idea of food, she who so endlessly devised it, made me think about her condition rather more seriously than I had hitherto. The fear that so obviously lurked in the minds of her sisters was once more palpable in the hot little room. Yet there were no outward signs of agitation, of concern. No nurse came in, there was as yet no chart at the foot of the bed, no equipment to remind one of the presence of surgeons, of doctors. It was just an ordinary little room, with a bed, a few chairs, and a rather unhelpfully strong light which shone directly on Dorrie's face. While Rosemary was unpacking a small offering of smoked salmon, I stole a look at Dorrie's ear. The lobe was red, but not distended: I could see no obvious lump. Perhaps there was a hard white speck in the surrounding red, but certainly nothing to distort the general shape. And anyway, I thought, if they had to do anything extensive, surely she would be in a hospital rather than in this oppressively silent place, where patients were stowed away behind doors whose cards proclaimed, 'The Hon. Mrs X., Mr Y.', and where the menus were so luxurious. Yet I

137

began to long for the presence of Oscar, who must surely know more about what was going on than any of us here.

'How is Oscar?' I asked.

'He'll be here in a moment, dear.' Dorrie smiled, as if the thought of her husband annihilated all anxiety. 'He just went out to get a new battery for my little radio.'

Poor Oscar, I thought, doomed forever to seek out electricians in hostile territory. There was a rattle of wheels in the corridor, and the door opened to reveal a maid with a supper tray. Immediately Janet and Rosemary got up, one to arrange pillows, the other to supervise the placing of the bed table. There was even an attempt, unbearable to my eyes, to raise Dorrie in the bed, as if she were incapable of doing so herself. So must they have played with dolls in their far-off childhood, and in turn with their baby sister, busying themselves with these important tasks that they had seen so often performed by adults. I think that they would even have spooned the soup into her mouth if she had let them. I could see that she would have to drink every drop, while they waited, their faces sharpened by anxiety, their eyes soft with love, to see if, while they so waited, her appetite had returned.

I was glad to note that this little rite of passage was successfully negotiated. The soup, and half of the omelette, were eaten, although the hand that played with the bread roll merely picked it to pieces, and the mouth trembled slightly. But who would not be nervous here, I asked myself, my foot in a spasm of cramp, my back to a radiator. And I doubted if she had been away from home for many years, certainly never to sleep in a strange bed, and alone. If she trembled, it was surely with fear of the night to come. Women of such simplicity, and here I included her sisters, were always unarmed before the prospect of solitude, frequently expressed their alarm at noises in the night, were

138

suspicious of strangers on their street, on their territory. It was left to my generation, and Heather's, of course, to exert an imperviousness to risk or danger that was perhaps not entirely felt. Women have come a long way, of course: we can all be left alone at night now. But sometimes it seems a high price to pay. We can also open the door cheerfully to strangers at any hour, deal with obscene telephone calls, and mend fuses. It has never occurred to me to wish that someone else would do the locking up, leaving me free to water the plants or make a last hot drink. It has never occurred to me because I do all these things as a matter of course. But Dorrie and her sisters still belonged to the protected variety, safe to express fear, anxiety, distress. Dorrie, I could see, although the youngest, was the strongest of the three. She was so used to absorbing the objections of others that she never thought of voicing any of her own, and was perhaps the better off for that reason, was certainly easier to live with. And perhaps she would come through this ordeal better than they would. Of course, I know one reads these terrible stories that anxiety stored is nefarious, that one should shout, scream, throw things at walls, 'express one's emotions' (when? where?) in order to avoid certain conditions that I refused to think about. After all, I was in line for them myself.

Oscar came in as Rosemary was trying to tempt Dorrie with the smoked salmon. 'You take it, Rachel,' she said in a disappointed voice. 'Eat it for supper. Have you got some brown bread at home?' That was another thing I liked about them, their concern for my next meal. Oscar bent over the bed and kissed Dorrie on the lips. She looked up at him as if all her fears had been laid to rest. 'It's all right, girls,' he said. 'I'll stay with her now. And here's Rachel. Nice to see you, dear.' He always noticed me, made me feel wanted. But it seemed to be the signal for us to leave, and the way that Dorrie clung to his hand made it obvious that they wanted to be alone together. They still had the air of a devoted, no, of an enamoured couple. That kiss on the lips had been fervent, exclusive of the rest of us. We rose from our chairs, as if in discretion, as if not to witness their communion. Kisses were planted on the forehead of a now placid Dorrie, scarves and gloves gathered, chairs placed back against the wall. Oscar had succeeded in turning that cruel light away from the bed and stood waiting for us to leave. The room now looked intimate, habitable. 'We'll see you tomorrow,' Janet said, subdued now with the implications of the separation to come. 'I'll be with Rose this evening, if you want anything.' 'We'll ring you later to say goodnight,' Rosemary said, mouthing to me behind Janet's back, 'She worries so. Better to put her mind at rest.' I waited politely outside the door, so that they could worry in concert for a few more minutes.

'Well, she looks quite comfortable,' said Janet sadly, when they at last joined me. Rosemary, her mouth drawn down at the corners, looked unlike her normally contentious self.

'I think you're both more worried than Dorrie is,' I rallied them. 'And I'm going to take you out and find you a hot cup of coffee. I think we all need one.'

They brightened at this, and we spent quite a pleasant half-hour in a café in Marylebone High Street. I gave a sturdy performance, in which I did not quite believe. When I saw them to their car, Rosemary kissed my cheek, and pressed the damp parcel of smoked salmon into my hand. 'So nice to see you, Rachel,' said Janet. 'Will we see you again?'

'Oh, I dare say I'll look in tomorrow,' I replied. 'If we're not too busy at the shop.' I waved casually and left them there in the dark street. It was difficult to imagine how they would spend the rest of the evening.

The following days saw us all in attendance. The

operation was delayed for some reason; nothing seemed to be happening, and gradually the atmosphere relaxed. Sometimes, sitting in that room, I could have persuaded myself that we were back in the drawing-room in Wimbledon, particularly when the husbands joined us, or when Oscar's brother, Sam, looked in, bringing with him the cold air of the street and a faint smell of cigars. Oscar said very little, but sat there, smiling faintly, as if in the enforced seclusion of these strange days he and Dorrie had been returned to their original love dream. And when he gave an almost imperceptible nod to his brother, we all obediently stood up to leave, bidding each other goodbye and promising to meet there the following day. But just when it seemed as if this might go on for ever, we heard that the operation was scheduled for the morning of the next day but one. Anxieties sharpened. Dorrie, her hand in Oscar's, looked trusting enough, but I noticed that she had spilled a little tea or coffee: there was a small pale brown stain on her pink bed-jacket. This told another story from her warm but tired smile. When I kissed her goodnight, promising to see her the following day, she raised herself in the bed and put her arms round me.

'Dear little Rachel,' she said. 'Get home safely.'

All of this put somewhat of a strain on my nerves. Although I fell almost restfully into those trance-like but convivial gatherings round the bedside, I began to wonder how well I would stand the pace if they were prolonged indefinitely. I particularly began to wonder how long it would be before Heather came home. By my calculations her weekend should be over by now, although of course she knew of no reason for hurrying back. It just seemed more and more incongruous that she had not been told, and that I was there in her place. I felt like the reserve in some key football match, accepted as a necessity, but with regret. I have to say that the others expressed no regret: I think they were genuinely

141

pleased that I was there. Strangely enough, Heather's name was not mentioned, but this was out of tact. I gathered that there had been some disagreement over the reasons for her absence. Janet, or Rosemary, probably Rosemary, had expressed strong disapproval that she should not be there, and Dorrie, of course, had defended her daughter. I imagined her becoming quite upset over Rosemary's remonstrances: I imagined agitation, tears coming into her eyes, Oscar intervening, Rosemary in retreat. Thereafter Heather's name was not mentioned, although whatever sadness was in the air was to do with her, her remoteness, physical in this case as well as mental, her unknowingness. Oscar's burdens must have been heavy at this time, knowing what he knew, yet not once did I hear him even sigh, courteous even in his preoccupation. There did seem to be a curious sort of dispensation hovering over the two of them, as they held hands like lovers, like children, so deeply attuned to each other that they even breathed in unison. With Oscar there, Dorrie would eat, and not just to please him either; Oscar was the first to notice that she was tired, even before she had realized it herself; Oscar gave us the signal to leave. But although it was clear that they had never been closer, I felt that Heather should have been there.

There was another reason for my longing for her return. Oscar and Dorrie had an air about them of fated lovers, and their passion was too naked for one of my sceptical persuasion. I felt that it should be kept within the family, although I trembled to think of its effect on Heather's benighted expectations. I also felt that the pronounced absence of Michael would inevitably come to public notice, and, knowing what I did, I did not want to be put in the position of having to divert enquiries or spread a smokescreen of polite ignorance whenever the subject was raised. In the event I found out that he was not expected to reappear; when his name

142

was mentioned, Janet and Rosemary shared an identical moue of distaste, while Sam surprised me by saying, 'How could you? I mean, how could you ever have taken him seriously?' The news had leaked out, or rather a sanitized version of it had been released; it was not that everybody knew everything, but that everybody knew something. Poor Michael, too readily accepted by his new relatives as a sort of part-timer, was now thought to be expendable. Indeed, their original affability had turned quite suddenly to a sort of tired impatience: it was as if they had bought an article which they thought they needed, had found it to be faulty, and could not wait to return it to the shop. Michael, I could see, would be returned to the custody of his father.

When I discovered that this attitude had been agreed upon, and was indeed shared, I was rather shocked. After all, it was one thing to marry an idiot, quite another to discard him after so short a term of trial. I judged this behaviour characteristic of the rich, and surprisingly cynical. I would not have expected it of them. But on reflection I saw that it had been urged upon them by fear. The fact of Dorrie's little illness had reminded them that Heather's place was with her mother. Indeed, the renewed, or perhaps perpetual, flowering of the love that Oscar and Dorrie had for one another seemed to call her home, as if any lesser emotion, any simulacrum, had no place in their scheme of things. I knew that beneath the placidity that each urged upon the other in those days at the Clinic they yearned for her. And if the end were approaching for them, then they had to have her back: her marriage, always an affair of convenience, had now become inconvenient, and must be cancelled as quickly as possible. It was a solution of sorts, I saw, and perhaps a clever move. For what Oscar and I knew – and I was sure that we were the only persons in that room who really knew what was wrong – could in fact never be

143

made public. Not one of them could have stood it.

I spared a thought for Michael and his effervescent father, but even I thought it better that we should be denied the opportunity of getting to know them further. I saw them endlessly drifting across the Spanish plains, or rather testing out the appurtenances of time-share apartments, bouncing on cheap mattresses, settling down in partly furnished rooms, calling irritably for mulish Spanish servants, banging down the telephone, their *bonhomie* resumed as soon as an acquaintance came into view. I believe they were immensely successful at what they did: at least money would be no problem. But their high-octane accessibility would surely decrease, giving way to the tired smiles of a pair of professional comedians. Or rather the father would assume this attitude: the son would be indulged, as if he really were a little retarded, whereas he was in fact seeking revenge for his spoilt childhood and would continue to exact forfeits. And the father would find his anxiety still intact, when he had thought to pass it on to others: he would become rueful, cynical, while obtaining his own pleasures when and where he could. His ladies would turn loud with annoyance as he habitually scuttled home to be with his son: they would profess amazement at the closeness of the bond, provide the names of psychiatrists, finally put up with it all – for he would choose women to whom not much more was likely to happen. The fact that we all disliked him seemed to me, if anything, to heighten his rather threadbare appeal. He was the real victim of this unfortunate affair, and it was hardly likely that he would seek the same solution on another occasion. He was, in effect, a doomed man.

But perhaps we were all doomed. The day before Dorrie was due to have her operation found us grouped around the bed, running out of blandishments, suddenly short of things to say. The tension was becoming acute, and Oscar and Dorrie mutely held hands for comfort. There was a sadness in the room, and also an impatience, a desire to yawn, fidget, talk in a loud voice, even to eat. The air was getting stale, still redolent of Dorrie's honeysuckle scent, but used up now, and mingled with the odour of her lunch, and the perpetual bedclothes. I found it intolerable. 'Dorrie,' I said. 'Wouldn't you like to take a turn in the corridor? I'm sure it's bad for you to be in bed all the time.' She turned her head to face me (surely the eyes were larger, the sockets a little more pronounced?) and over my shoulder looked towards the door, which at that moment opened to admit Heather.

The great smile that burst upon Dorrie's face told me what had happened before I confronted the cause for it. There was a general murmur of congratulation, as if the curtain had just gone up on an amazing spectacle. Oh, well done, I thought, perhaps a little sourly: the prodigal returns.

'Hello, Mummy,' she said. 'What have you been getting up to? Gosh, it's hot in here.' And she moved over and opened a window, something that none of us had dared to do.

In contrast to the rest of us, who were by now a little sickly, she looked marvellously well. She was wearing her chestnut suit and had a small purse on a long strap, obviously Italian, over her chest like a bandolier. She was different, somehow, or maybe it was the effect of coming into this room from the wider world. She was assured and businesslike, not a bit perturbed by the spectacle of us all sitting like mutes: either that, or she was putting on a good show.

'Darling, darling,' said Dorrie, holding out her arms. 'Are you all right? Aren't you cold? How could you, darling, coming out without a coat?'

'Of course I'm all right,' Heather replied in her usual monotone, but pitched a little more heartily, which

145

gave her a certain curatorial authority. 'And you're all right, too. At least you will be after tomorrow.'

'Yes, dear, of course I'm all right.' She looked it. She looked as if health had returned to her quite suddenly. 'Oh, I can't wait to get this over and to be at home. Ring the bell, Oscar. Let's have some tea.'

'Oh, don't bother, Daddy. I'll find someone.' She nodded to me almost imperceptibly, and I followed her to the door.

'That's right, dear,' said Dorrie. 'You two girls have a nice talk. Oh, I feel so much better now. I knew she'd come.'

As the door swung to behind me I could hear the others reassuring themselves that, of course, they knew she'd come. She had timed it beautifully. I followed her along the corridor, saw her summon a nurse out of thin air, and order tea as if she were in charge of the whole party.

'Terrific,' I said. 'How did you know?'

'Daddy rang me at the Gritti. By the way, you can always get hold of me there. Or leave a message. I call in most days.'

'But why should I want to get hold of you there?' I asked, in some surprise. 'You're home now.'

'Yes, but I'm going back. As soon as this is over. As soon as she's out of here.'

We were standing in a long grey corridor, with unhelpful strip lighting. From the far end came a rattle of wheels, as a maid appeared with a trolley of chattering tea cups.

'Going back?' I said. 'But you can't go back. Surely your place is here.'

'I don't know,' she said. 'The fact is, I've met someone. Come on. They'll wonder what's keeping us.'

I contemplated her stylish back in stupefaction. My indignation was rising rapidly to the surface, although I

146

knew that the polite fictions had to be sustained for as long as this little adventure had to run its course.

'Just a minute,' I said, catching up with her outside the door. 'What about Michael?' I found myself whispering furiously.

'Oh, he's gone,' she replied in her normal voice. 'I told him I was leaving him and he didn't seem surprised. Just packed his clothes and left. I'm putting the flat on the market.'

Heather's entrance, *en coup de vent*, had had a galvanizing effect on the assembly. She was complimented on her appearance and congratulated, as if she were a royal visitor, bestowing benefits by her magic presence. Her clothes were remarked upon, and she was invited to tell them what was being worn in Italy that season. Once again she claimed the attention, as she had during those far-off days when she had admitted, without any inflection of voice or behaviour, that her life had taken a decisive turn. I saw now that it was she who had done all the deciding, and I wondered whether the same phenomenon was being re-enacted. I saw, as in some paralysing dream, that I might have to stay here for ever, leaving Heather to pursue her plans in Italy. Apart from the fact that I had no wish to sacrifice myself in this matter, I had no more reason to trust her judgement on this occasion than I had previously, when events had proved her to be so stunningly wrong. I was inclined to see the present object of her attention as equally unworthy: not a gondolier, exactly – she was too stately and immovable for so vulgar an attachment – but certainly no one she could possibly bring home. The thought occurred to me that she might wish to enact this liaison far from the eyes of her family circle, and that thought should have alerted me to the possible seriousness of the affair, as should her new assurance. Silence, exile, and cunning, James Joyce's desiderata for an artist's life, seemed to have been discovered by

147

Heather with the rapidity and the inevitability of one who led a charmed existence.

I must confess to feeling furious with her. In addition to the sheer inconvenience of it all, I felt that Heather had usurped my independence and was in effect using my time to enjoy the equivalent of my habitual adventures. And, I thought, once she realized that such adventures were preferable to more complex and burdensome attachments, who knew what path she might not follow? But over and above my fury I felt a pang of pity for this slow-moving girl, with her prudish good manners, and her awakening in the arms of a knowing Italian, the word passed round behind her unsuspecting back. Gradually she would assume a puzzled and preoccupied air, although her inward thoughts would take on a darker colouring. What happens to women is that they never entirely lose the faith that it will all come out right in the end, that the next man, or the next, will be the answer to their original expectations of stability and order, will resolve the difficult equation of innocence and experience. She was not made for my sort of life. She did not have the mental equipment, the reserves of temperament, the cynicism, the taste for danger. I saw her in years to come, living out her obedient life with her parents, and escaping to her adventures abroad, a child at home, a schemer, a pragmatist, far from loving eyes. She would become one of those efficient women in the rag trade, disaffectedly reviewing fashions, looked on for tips to current trends. Time and age would happen to her, bulking out her already sturdy figure, fading her hair, and the vision still far off, waiting to be sought. I could see her in her parents' drawing-room in years to come, a little untidy round the hips, a little weary, still polite, still private, as she tended their now wistful expectations, parrying their questions, giving no hint. It was no life for a decent woman, and yet it is the life that many

148

women have had to lead. And it is the lot of such women to be despised, as if they had failed some essential test, the test that more fortunate women have had the wit to pass. No sign of love would appear to change that changeless expression, and eventually she would find herself indispensable to her friends, as reflector, as recipient of confidences, as baby-sitter, as flavour enhancer of safer and more recognized conditions. No amount of transient lovers would redeem her status. She would be referred to as 'poor Heather'. And women of a more conventional stripe would feel gloriously sorry for her.

Nevertheless, she had no business to adopt this career at this inconvenient moment, ill-equipped as she was, and with the blundering goodwill that characterized her. She should give it up, I felt, recognize her limitations, stay within her boundaries. She had money, she had the status of a married woman – still important, even in these liberated days – and she had a career of sorts. And she had a home to which she could always return. The true adventuress knows that she can never go home again. That was the essential difference between us. I felt that Heather was making the most enormous miscalculation and that she was making it at other people's expense. Yet even now I had to give her credit for her performance. Not for Heather the dropped hint, the larky raised eyebrows, that would signify to the world at large that something of an amorous nature was afoot. She had at least learned the first lesson; she had learned to keep her own counsel. She answered all the questions readily, but with no show of enthusiasm. Yes, she had bought one or two things; yes, it had been tiring; yes, she and Chiara had been glad to get to the Gritti; yes, she had known Chiara for some time, had met her mother, and her brother, Marco. They apparently lived in a rather modest way, and Chiara had been delighted with Oscar's offer of a luxurious weekend. By the end of her recital, her parents and her aunts were almost ready to adopt Chiara and her family as old friends, much as they had swum unsuspectingly into the open arms of Colonel Sandberg. No, said Heather, Chiara was not thinking of visiting London: she was too busy with her own little shop. But they kept in touch. What a pity, they all said: we should have so liked to meet her.

I suspected this Chiara, but by this time I suspected practically everybody. My ill will had reached such proportions that I silently accused them all of complicity, of making things too easy for her. But there was no doubt that she had transformed the situation. Among the tea cups an air of expectation reigned. Even the operation seemed a thing of little importance. The general feeling seemed to be a desire to get it out of the way so that life could resume its normal appearance, and all be as before, with Heather in attendance once more. Dorrie was cheerful now, and had her normal colour in her cheeks. When Sam came in, on his way home, welcomes and good wishes had to be repeated. We were all surprised when we saw how late it was.

It was a nurse who told us to leave. The long night of preparation was about to begin. I kissed Dorrie and told her that I would telephone the following day, and would come back when it was all over. I waited outside the door, hoping to catch Heather, for now my curiosity was aroused. It was difficult, and it would have looked too obvious, to detach her from her father at this stage, yet I did manage to have a word with her. It seemed surreal, in that corridor, to ask her whom, in particular, she had met. 'Oh, I'll give you a call,' she said, infuriatingly. 'Before I go back.'

N I N E

WHEN I telephoned the Clinic the following afternoon, I was told that Mrs Livingstone had had
her operation but was still sedated. Her husband was
with her, but no other visitors would be allowed. I was
advised to telephone again later.

I was a little surprised that such a curfew should be
imposed. I had thought that the actual surgery would
take about half an hour at the most, and would be
followed by a quick recovery and a rapid discharge. The
whole thing was proving to be more cumbersome than I
imagined. But I supposed that the anxiety of her family
had prevailed and that they had agreed to turn this little
episode into a sort of rest cure, to which no time limits
need be attached. Indeed, the current mythology was
that Dorrie was 'exhausted', and that explanations were
not difficult to find. That disastrous marriage had 'worn
her out'; she was 'prostrated' by the outcome, although
curiously enough nobody seemed to want to take any
responsibility for this. The fabled preparations for the
wedding, the wedding itself, were seen as a manifesta-
tion of family virtue, of unselfishness, of generosity,
even of chivalry, and I suppose that this was more or
less true. The brute fact of the rapid dissolution of the
marriage itself was viewed with distaste, as if it were
happening to somebody else. If pressed to examine this
attitude a little more closely, the consensus of the sisters
would have been that Michael had proved unreliable,
that his background was eccentric, and that he had failed
to settle down. Heather would emerge from this im-
broglio as if from a convent, with not a stain on her
character.

All this was so near the truth – which only Oscar and

I possessed – that it was found to be generally acceptable, even comfortable. I was not alone in noticing the
fine web of deceit thus thrown over the affair, for I had
seen Oscar turning his face reflectively to the window
from time to time, as if taking a brief sabbatical from
family unanimity. The same cosmetic procedure
seemed to have overtaken the business of Dorrie's ear,
which did not in itself, as far as I could see, require
prolonged bed rest. My general irritability on this score
contained a quantum of fear, certainly, but also of
impatience. How the rich succumbed to their ailments!
And how premature this prostration would be when
news of Heather's little divagations came into greater
prominence! Would her imminent departure be greeted
with the same indulgence as her forthcoming uncon-
tested divorce? Would the same euphemisms be used to
describe what was only too obviously a foreign adventure of the most banal kind? And would these euphemisms eventually die on the lips when that adventure was
repeated at regular intervals?

If, on the other hand, Dorrie were really ill, then
Heather's temporary defection would be overlooked,
forgotten, cancelled, in the relief of her having returned
to deal with the situation. Indeed, it would be a matter
of urgency to secure Heather's continued presence even
before that presence was officially required. As so often
in my relations with the Livingstones, I now reflected
that I had done all I could, or, unfortunately, nearly all:
my supreme, my ultimate task would be to talk sense to
Heather, persuade her, in my own inimitable way, that
what awaited her in Venice could be postponed *sine die*
(could indeed be renewed or replicated at a time to suit
her in the future) and that it would be more seemly on
her part to inaugurate a period of official spinsterhood
until the time was propitious for her next brief dis-
appearance. This would be a matter of convenience all
round, I would explain: I would not harp on the fact

that fears for Dorrie's health could not be entirely discounted, but would take the line that the life she was about to embark upon required a coolness of attitude and a long-term strategy that she would do better to contemplate, perhaps in the comfort of her now deserted flat, before succumbing to its more obvious pitfalls. To this end I telephoned her, hoping to catch her before she left for the hospital to be with her father when Dorrie came round from her anaesthetic.

Having to see her was, as always, inconvenient, but time was short, both the time allowed for the interview and the time I could spare from the shop, where business was suddenly booming and Robin was beginning to look a little frayed. It was a sense of my own position that led me to force the issue. I set out for Marble Arch on one of those gloomy days that threaten rain but never deliver it, fearful, despite myself, of those lowering clouds and what they concealed. The events of the previous days had put me into such a state of nervous receptivity that my hydrophobia seemed to darken the edges of my mind and even the sight of Robin pouring glass after glass of water down his throat made me uneasy. I found myself glancing upwards at the dark grey sky, as I hastened along the Bayswater Road, willing it to remain dry until I reached the safe anchorage of Heather's flat. There I would deliver my message as expeditiously as possible before hurrying back to my own four walls. It is when I am in this state that I have bad dreams. All of this was an additional burden to me.

Heather opened the door and stood politely aside to let me into her flat. She seemed to have no idea why I should wish to see her, but was, as ever, wordlessly accommodating. I felt it was appropriate to remain standing while I pointed out the error of her ways, and she, with her invincible politeness, remained standing with me. She was not an inventive girl and had no

153

thought of making me comfortable. I was grateful for this for there was no way in which I could feel comfortable in my decision to do what clearly had to be done. Indeed, as we stood there in the hallway of her silent flat, a clock ticking monotonously somewhere in the background, I could feel the familiar tide of exasperation rising to the full.

'Heather,' I said, gamely. 'You mentioned that you were going back to Venice, and I don't think you should.'

'Why not?' she asked.

'Well, apart from the fact that your mother is ill, I think your timing is wrong.'

She looked at me, with that familiar amiable blankness in her face. Clearly I was going to get no help from her. I tried again.

'You mentioned that you had met someone and I rather gathered that you were going back to see him. Or to be with him.'

'That's right. Marco. Marco Barbieri.'

I was momentarily diverted. 'Marco? Chiara's brother?'

'Yes.'

'But Heather,' I said, rather more gently. 'Surely you can visit your friend at any other time?'

'You don't understand,' she replied. She was rather pale now. 'We love one another. We're going to be married.'

'Oh, come on, Heather. You *are* married. Surely once is enough? You've got all this,' I gestured towards the chandelier, the only emblem of 'all this' I could find available. 'Why not stay here and make the best of it? You can visit him in due course. Of course you can. Or he can come here. Why can't he do that?'

'You don't understand,' she repeated. 'He can't leave. He supports his widowed mother. I shall have to live there.'

'With his widowed mother? In Venice?'

'Well, of course.'

She seemed to take it for granted that I would accept this, as she had apparently done, with no show of resistance.

'Look,' I said. 'I don't want to be unkind but I think you set too much store by marriage. After all, you went into marriage with Michael as if it were the most natural thing in the world that you should. And it hasn't worked out, has it.'

'No,' she said. 'But you see, I love Marco.'

'Well, then,' I exploded. 'Why not just love him? It can be done, you know. You don't have to marry everyone. In fact I think you should steer clear of marriage. And I can't see you living with anybody's widowed mother in Venice. The whole idea is preposterous. Your place is here.'

She said nothing, but merely rested her hand for support on a console table. I remember looking at her reflection in the mirror that hung above it. She was back in her black garments, for some reason, a loose sweater and a long jersey skirt, that made my heavy raincoat feel oppressive by comparison. Her hair was cut short again, and a long strand lay across her forehead. She seemed to me to be dressed in mourning clothes, or in the clothes appropriate to a Venetian daughter-in-law. I revised my earlier estimate of her future career.

'Look here,' I said, in some alarm. 'Don't do anything stupid. You can have your love affair. After all, you have money. If money is a problem there . . .' My voice trailed away, as she turned to me in some amusement. Now I lost the reflection of her in the mirror as she moved towards me out of its range.

'Rachel,' she said. 'Why are you saying all this? My mind is quite made up, you know.'

'Because you are in danger of marrying a man whom you have just met,' I said grimly. 'Just as you did

155

before. And marriage is not the answer to everything, you know. Some women are just not meant to marry.'

'And some women are,' she replied. 'I am. I always wanted to be married, even when I was a little girl. I wanted to be married and to stay married, like my parents. I want children. I want a home.'

'You've got a home,' I said meanly, thinking of my hard-earned flat. 'You've got two homes. You can always go back to your parents.'

'I only want one home,' she said. 'I want my husband's home.'

'But you're going to make the same mistake again! Look here, Heather, I know you're inexperienced, but this is ridiculous.' I sat down. 'Don't you know that you can fall in love again and again, and that it doesn't always work out? Don't you realize that in these situations it is up to you to stand clear? To keep a cool head? To preserve yourself?'

'Like you?' she asked, still politely.

'Well, yes, why not? I manage. In fact I do very well. Of course, I haven't had your advantages,' I said, breathing rather hard. 'I can't cancel everything the minute it all goes wrong, as you are apparently prepared to do. I haven't got loving parents who think everything I do is right, even if it isn't. I have to live by the light of reason. I'm not saying it isn't hard. I'm just saying it can be done. And reason means being grown up, even a little sceptical. Reason means not having weddings every five minutes, with new clothes, and people giving you presents, as if you were still a little girl. Reason means doing it the hard way, keeping quiet, being discreet. Reason means having the strength to do without.'

'You make it sound terrible,' she said.

'It is terrible,' I burst out. 'But who said life wasn't terrible? People like you seem to think it is a sort of party, to which invitations are sent out. People like you don't seem to realize when the celebrations have to stop. Or that not everybody gets to go to this party of yours. Some of us have to *work*,' I said. 'Stay buoyant. Stay purposeful. Stay smiling, and helpful, and *solvent*. People like us are braver than people like you will ever be. And, frankly, I think I am years ahead of you. I know what I need, to be all these things, *and* clear-headed, *and* useful. Women don't sit at home any more, you know, dreaming of Prince Charming. They don't do it because they've found out that he doesn't exist. As you should have found out. I live in the real world, the world of deceptions. You live in the world of illusions. That is one of the differences between us. Another one is that I don't choose to go public every five minutes. What I do is my own affair and nobody else's. Of course, it's terrible,' I said, with some passion. 'But you see, I've found out that there are no easy options.'

'I didn't say it would be easy.' A very small flicker of trouble crossed her face.

'Oh, but you believe it will be.' Nothing would stop me now. 'Women like you, protected, sentimental, spoilt, how could you possibly envisage difficulty? You have no conception of it, the height, the depth, the *duration* of it. Listen, Heather, I wanted to get married once. Of course I did. But he was married, and nobody made it easy for me. Yes, I thought like you once. I wanted the same things. But since then . . . Well, he taught me a lot. He taught me to take care of myself, to give away nothing I couldn't spare. He taught me to see to it that I was the one in control. That's a grim lesson to have to learn. But I learnt it. And I'm still here. And I'm not likely to end up supporting someone else's widowed mother in the back streets of Venice, miles from home.'

'You'll have to excuse me,' she said. 'I rather want to get to the hospital. I'd give you a lift, but you're going in the opposite direction.'

'And what about your parents?' I went on. 'Have you

told them? And are they prepared to bail you out once again? Oh, you make me despair. Why do you think I came here? I'm trying to tell you not to do anything final, not to throw everything away. There are other men. There are always other men. You may not like the idea but I can promise you that you will come to terms with it. You will have to. I had to. Again and again and again. But it need not be a death sentence, you know. You may even learn to enjoy it. In fact, you may have to. Your entire future may depend on it. I know, I know. Women like you are squeamish about things like that. But who said it was all a fairy tale? Women like you or women like me?'

She collected her keys from the table and put them in her bag.

'Shall we go?' she said, opening the door and standing aside to let me pass.

Without noticing how this had happened, I found myself on the pavement outside the entrance, feeling bulky and superfluous in my raincoat and still breathing irregularly after my outburst. I was, at some level of consciousness, aware of Heather stealing silently away in her flat black shoes after glancing at me once more, with her usual adamantine amiability. I felt exhausted and ashamed, as one always does after any kind of confession. But someone has to say these things. Someone has to point out to people of Heather's imperviousness that there are a few duties connected with being an adult in an adult world. Except that I wished that it did not have to be people like me that issued the warning. I felt the old sickening sense of loss that privileged people always visit on me. It is a peculiar sort of love affair that I have with them. I want to be like them, yet at the same time I want to be taken under their wing, into their protection. And this can never be. For such people know, even before I do, that I am not like them. They are very sorry but the fact is ineluctable. I had seen something of that in Heather's face while I had been trying to bring her to her senses. That look was to return to me frequently in the course of the afternoon. I felt disconsolate and downgraded, but that is sometimes the price one pays for standing one's ground. There seemed to be no answer to any of it.

But it was clear that I could not attempt to come to terms with Heather again, nor could I even face her. That look of hers, as if she could not hear anything that I had been saying, was enough to warn me. I felt that I had lost her, and that the loss was entirely my fault, which was ridiculous, because what I had been trying to do was preserve that little family in all its pristine innocence, the quality that had attracted me to them in the first place. I still felt that it was absurd of her to embark on a romantic adventure at this particular juncture, to pretend that everything would be all right, when it so clearly would not, to abandon home, obligations, duty, loyalty, just at the moment when they would be most needed. Her plans were so impractical that someone like me was necessary to point this out. But it was precisely people like me who had no credibility in her eyes. Her particular form of nurturing made someone like me sound unrealistic, as if my entire formation were out of order. And I saw, sadly, I must admit, that she had not considered my words to be at all serious – not frivolous, exactly, but out of court, off bounds, disreputable. She would never grow up, never make the right decisions. She would drift calmly from one disaster to another, never thinking that there might be an alternative, and that the answer might lie within her buried powers. Her famous shrewdness had quite deserted her. And in the meantime there was her mother to consider. I envisaged, with a further sinking of the heart, that first hesitant stirring from the anaesthetic, and all the bad news that was waiting to greet Dorrie as she endeavoured to gather her forces

159

together for the task of recovery.

I wandered listlessly back to the shop, where other, more practical, duties awaited me. My life suddenly seemed effortful: I suppose I was rather tired. I felt as I had felt after those storms of childhood, when, with tears, I had begged for forgiveness. How right I had been, I thought, to steer clear of all those weakening emotions, to sail free. And when I eventually saw the lights of the shop – for it was already dark: I must have been gone for some time, must in fact have delayed Heather – I was glad once again to have all those other duties awaiting me. Robin, harassed, merely nodded to me as I slipped in. I took off my coat and joined him, and stayed there until six o'clock. Trade was brisk, and we did not even have time to make a cup of tea.

Perhaps I had pitched it too high, I thought, as my spirits slowly returned in those few moments of quiet after I had locked up. Perhaps I should have spoken more gently. But by the same token, perhaps something had sunk in. One could not always temper the wind to the shorn lamb. And perhaps shorn lambs were not there to be eternally preserved in their unknowingness. Perhaps they too must take their chance in the great game. No protection, after all, was guaranteed for life. And if, in her very slowness, Heather had not reacted to my diatribe, that same slowness might ensure that in due course she would think about what I had said. It would not matter much if her opinion of me declined somewhat. I had the impression that she had never taken me entirely seriously. In which case there was no real shame attached to what had taken place. I had remained in character and so had she. I could not on that account join her in her fantasies, nor would I be expected to. The more I thought about it, the more I realized that I could not have acted otherwise. My spirits rapidly returning to normal, I put the kettle on. I remembered that I had not eaten any lunch.

There was no need for me to go to the hospital: one more visit, when Dorrie was convalescent, would see the matter concluded. One more telephone call was required of me that day and then I would relinquish the field, leaving them all to work out Heather's destiny. I dialled the number of the Clinic and asked for Mrs Livingstone.

'Who's calling, please?'

'Rachel Kennedy.'

'Are you a relative?'

'Why, no,' I said, in some surprise. This was the first time I had encountered such formalities. 'Just a friend.'

'Mrs Livingstone is not too well. Her husband and daughter are with her. She is not allowed any other visitors.'

'Just a minute,' I interrupted. 'Has she had her operation?'

'The operation was successful, but she has a slight temperature. Perhaps you could call tomorrow.' The telephone was put down before I had a chance to say any more.

I sat down slowly. The kettle boiled, and I got up and turned off the gas. Then I put on my coat, picked up my bag, and left the flat.

It was raining steadily now. I seemed to know, even at that stage, that I would not be returning home that evening. My heart was beating strongly and I wanted to walk in order to defuse my sense of alarm, but a taxi seethed along beside me and I stopped it. Waves of water seemed to part under its wheels, and the street lights had frayed whitish edges. Submerged in the taxi's dark little cave I watched the meter, not because I thought I might not have enough money on me but because it was the only thing I could see clearly. Rain spattered diagonally on the windows and we were held up interminably at Marble Arch. Then the traffic all seemed to disappear and soon we were proceeding,

161

much too inexorably, it seemed to me, up the dark defile of Wimpole Street.

At the Clinic, on Dorrie's floor, it was so silent that I seemed to hear the hum of the strip lighting. There was an oxygen cylinder outside her door. I knocked softly, and because there was no response I went in. In an instantaneous impression, the affair of a split second, I saw Dorrie under a film of plastic, her hair plastered to the sides of her face. She looked as if she were drowning.

'No, no,' said Oscar, half rising from the bed. 'Don't come in.'

I retreated to the passage, putting the door between myself and that dreadful image. In that same split second I had seen Heather, sitting, in her black garments, her head bowed, holding her mother's hand. In the half hour or so that I spent outside I seemed to see Oscar rising continually from the bed, his face grey, his arm flung out in warning, or in remonstrance. I felt returned to childhood, when my mother was ill, sensing momentous happenings behind a terrible door. It was shockingly quiet. I stayed there, leaning against the wall, until I heard footsteps. Two doctors were coming down the corridor, and simultaneously, from the lift, Janet and Rosemary appeared. They looked a hundred years old as they clung to each other for comfort.

The door opened again, and I heard, 'Try her with the mask.' One of the doctors came out and summoned a porter to wheel in the oxygen cylinder. There was a brief flurry of activity, and Janet and Rosemary went into the room. In the instant before the door swung to again I saw Oscar holding the mask to Dorrie's face. She bent forward into it as if to vomit.

Not to be included was awful to me, and yet I knew that I had no part in this except as a witness. My part, perhaps the hardest, was to wait, alone, without news, and without the right to interfere. So I waited, which

162

was all I could do, leaning against the wall in the corridor, sometimes walking to the end, my steps silent on the rubber floor, the humming lights my only companions. At some point Janet and Rosemary came out, in tears, and I thought it must all be over; it appeared, however, that there was a brief lull, that Dorrie was now dozing. But the outlook was grave, and they would not leave. They would not have left anyway: the problem would have been to keep them away. When a nurse appeared with a trolley full of instruments they sprang forward in alarm.

'What is happening?' cried Rosemary hoarsely. 'What are they going to do?'

'Mr Hill may want to perform a tracheotomy,' was the reply, and once more the door closed.

We stayed there all night, although night and day were one under those lights, in that silence. When the nurse came out with the trolley, she was followed by a man who had to be Mr Hill. He held up his hands, as if to ward off our questions. 'She is very ill,' he said flatly. 'But she is breathing more easily. Nothing more can be done tonight. You might as well go home.'

Suddenly I felt faint and I knew that I must get out into the air. I kissed the sisters, who embraced me fervently in return. We clasped hands, as if reluctant to part. Then I was out in the mournful street, still dark, still wet, and utterly unpeopled. I remember ploughing my way through the deserted city like a sleepwalker, and when I got home I either fell into a real sleep or passed out: a sudden descent into blackness. When I woke up it was beginning to be day but all my lights were still on. I felt quite numb but I had recovered a little energy. I remembered to make a hot drink before I started back to the Clinic.

Incredibly, I saw a maid going into Dorrie's room with a cup of tea. I thought this insensitive, to say the least, until I saw the smile on her face when she emerged. 'You can go in,' she said. 'But don't stay. Amazing, isn't it.' I went in. Dorrie lay back on mountainous pillows, sipping from a cup held to her lips by Oscar.

'Rachel,' she said. Her voice was a harsh whisper.

'What happened?'

'You had a bad night,' I said. 'But it's over now. How do you feel?'

'Tired.' She turned her great eyes to me. 'Were you here?'

'Oscar and Heather were with you,' I said.

'Oh, I know.' She smiled beatifically. 'I'm so lucky.' Then she drifted into sleep.

All wrongs were righted; nothing was irretrievable. I left them there and walked back to the shop in a state of extraordinary lightness. It was seven-thirty: the traffic was already building up. I had a bath, made something to eat, and went down to open the shop.

In the days that followed it seemed as if all the unpleasantness had been a dream. Drawn back to that room in spite of myself, I was present at the joyful reunions, of sister with sister, with brothers-in-law, with nieces. Oscar and Heather were there all the time, their extreme fatigue apparent not in their faces, which were polite masks, but in their inability to say anything. I marvelled at their supreme tact; not for a moment did Dorrie know how ill she had been. As time passed, and she returned to normal, her nerves unaffected by that night when she had come so near to death and of which she had no memory, it seemed as though a general tide of euphoria were sweeping her on to full health. The room filled up once more with flowers: bottles of champagne were produced, toasts were drunk, laughter was heard. Eagerly, the sisters watched her appetite, which soon became surprisingly good. Every meal eaten was a cause for congratulation. It was just that occasionally, when she would lay down her spoon, she

164

would look round obediently, perhaps a little puzzled, and then she would catch my eye and smile. For some reason I felt like a murderer. I saw then that any infraction of the liberty of such simple people would be a form of assault. I saw then that I might have hurt Heather; not hurt her feelings, exactly, but damaged her innocence. I would have to put this right somehow, but at the same time I would have to convince her that her defection could not now take place. My part in all her plans seemed to be a nasty one, but, surely, having seen what she had seen, and having endured what she had endured, she could not now leave her mother to face her life without her, when, with her, she had managed to overcome the last enemy.

Hollow phrases rang in my head, for I was not required to say much in that room where only compliments and euphemisms were in order. In comparison I seemed to appear to myself as a creature of blunt brute instincts, put into the world in order to point out the facts of the emperor's new clothes: a necessary function but hardly a popular one. And yet I could not reconcile myself to merely being a silent Greek chorus: I was perfectly willing to supply the commentary, but I wanted to have some effect on the action. Unlike the others in that room, I found it enormously difficult to pretend that nothing had happened. These are the facts, I wanted to say; death comes swiftly. And it usually comes too soon, while mourning is endless. Very few can negotiate a stay of execution. The gathering of rosebuds may be recommended, but this is largely a peacetime occupation: for those who have received the warning graver considerations must obtain. I felt like that watchman in the Bible, who is supposed to blow a trumpet when danger approaches, knowing all the time that it is easy to ignore the sound, particularly when it is inconvenient, or when pleasurable expectations are aroused. It is the fate of the watchman not to be heard,

165

but unless he does his job he has no other justification.

I wondered how to negotiate Heather's recall to order, which somehow had to be mingled with an apology and an excuse that I perhaps had learned too much of the world and she too little. This seemed to me imperative: I did not want any lack of consideration to lie on my conscience, but at the same time I knew that her mother would really die without her, and perhaps her father too, but die of a broken heart, that heart they had in common where Heather was concerned. I did not at the time think that any of this was melodramatic. Looking back much later I came to see it as something from the pages of a nineteenth-century novel, yet such was the power of these people, so untouched were they by the wickedness of the world, that one was drawn into their triumphs and their tragedies as if by a superior force. I suppose that they made me conscious of the loss of my own innocence, and for that reason I tried to behave well, for good behaviour was what distinguished them, and perhaps distinguished them from me. For that reason I did not want Heather to indulge in the sort of activities in which I might have caught myself. It became imperative for me to secure her continuance in the only role for which she seemed best fitted, and for which she had no doubt been born.

When we heard that Dorrie could go home in a few days' time, it became a matter of urgency for me to take Heather on one side. I did not relish my task, but I saw opportunities diminishing once we were no longer brought together at Dorrie's bedside. Throughout the ordeal Heather had preserved her almost abstract polite-ness, had welcomed me as a visitor, even sometimes as a friend, although she was so restrained that it was difficult to tell what she really felt. It was noticeable, at least it was noticeable by me, that she made no attempt to take me aside in order to justify herself. There was no hint of a consciousness of recidivism in her behaviour.

166

But then, I told myself, her behaviour had never given anything away, and she was too superior to drop hints. This superiority did impress me as genuine. All amiability, but an amiability which committed her to nothing, and to no one person as opposed to another, she was a tribute to her parents' upbringing, and also to her own strength of character.

When I finally managed to get her to myself and to propose a cup of coffee, she assented as if we had parted on the best of terms. In fact it was I who felt vaguely culpable. We walked decorously to that same café in Marylebone High Street where I had lately sat with her aunts, and I watched her anxiously as she ate two cakes with an apparently unaffected appetite. Her nervous equilibrium seemed proof against any contingency.

'Heather,' I said. 'I wanted to tell you how marvellous I think you've been.'

'Oh, no, not really,' she replied. 'I did what I had to. But it's nice of you to say so. And nice of you to come so regularly. I know it has meant a lot to Mummy.'

'It was wonderful that you managed to be here,' I said. 'What would have happened if you had been away doesn't bear thinking about.' There was a pause, during which she touched the corners of her mouth with a paper napkin. 'You won't be going away now, I suppose?' I said, for this was what I was there to say.

'Oh, yes, I'll still be going. Not for a couple of weeks, of course. Not until she's properly better.'

'But Heather, this is a little precipitate. She's been very ill, you know. She may need you.'

'I don't think you've understood me, Rachel. Of course she may need me. She may always need me. But I can't always be here.'

Wearily, I prepared to go all through it again. My arguments sounded stale even to me. Yet, as if to spare me, and I did at the time think that she was being remarkably forbearing, she said, 'Don't trouble yourself. I know what I am going to do. I always have.'

It was the note of condescension in her voice that made me angry. I tried once more. 'It's not just your mother. Your father is exhausted. He can't bear all this by himself. He is not a young man. And you really should be here for him, you know. How could they possibly manage without you?' I thought it better not to dwell on the real reason for her decision, but I could not refrain from asking her how long she had known this Marco. If it was a brief acquaintance, then my arguments would have a certain weight; if not, then I would have to think again.

'How long have you known him?' I asked.

'Oh, not long,' she said. 'In fact I only met him last month.'

I stared at her. 'And you're prepared to risk your whole future, and everybody else's, on someone you hardly know?'

'Oh, yes.'

'And live with his mother? Incidentally, why can't your friend Chiara support her?'

'Well, you see, Chiara is getting married.' She drained the last of her coffee.

Oh, these weddings, I thought. They are all in love with them. As soon as one marries, the next one has to: it is an affair of honour. And all weddings must be well aspected: it is the rule. This attitude seemed to me to be so benighted that I seriously thought of saying my piece all over again. But something in her face, something of her mother's expression, stopped me. And she must be very tired, I thought. She probably isn't very rational at the moment. I was tired myself, and Christmas loomed, which, at the shop, meant total exhaustion. She certainly wouldn't leave before Christmas. I would have time to try again.

T E N

THE pre-Christmas rush passed in a blur of hard
work, late nights and strained nerves. We had a
good season but were all overtired by the end of it. We
said a final goodbye to Eileen, who promised to help
out on a part-time basis if either of us wanted to go
away on holiday; then Robin went off to his sister in the
country, leaving me alone in the shop on Christmas
Eve. The atmosphere was mildly frenzied, and then
suddenly, at about five o'clock, it went dead. Streets
cleared, traffic dwindled, and only the supermarkets
were doing any business. I stayed open until six, then
thankfully locked up and went upstairs. I would not see
Robin again until he came back for stocktaking at the
end of the month.

I slept a good deal over the holiday, waking only in
time to have a bath, get dressed, and go out in the
evening. I found myself enjoying this half-way existence, devoted only to sleep and amusement. So must
certain women have lived in days gone by, I reflected,
before it was decreed that hard work was to be their
portion. I am not against work; I have worked hard all
my life. But I found this courtesan's deportment rather
agreeable, and it seemed to me that if I had the choice,
and the money, of course, I might choose not to work
so hard, or rather not to choose work as my vocation. I
thought to myself that if I gave it another ten years, I
might well decide not to buy the shop myself but to sell
my share to Robin, and just decamp, disappear, lie in
the sun somewhere, out of touch, out of reach. This
plan, which had so far only been a fantasy, began to take
on the lineaments of reality. I could see myself putting
up the sign saying CLOSED on the door and slipping

169

away, never to reappear.

I did not think that anyone would miss me, nor would I leave very much behind in the way of commitments. I could abandon the flat without regret, much as one leaves an hotel room at the end of a holiday. All I would need would be a ticket to the sun. After all, the beauty of my kind of life is that it can be lived anywhere. Whatever it lacks in acquisitions it makes up for in variety, in volatility, in independence. Not everyone can deal with this. Among my women friends I have noticed one or two wilting under the strain, however brave and resolute they are in pursuit of their own form of fulfilment, the kind we are told to value these days. These are the ones who would secretly have been happier sitting at home listening to Woman's Hour, but instead are to be found on the city streets early in the morning, tapping their way along the pavement in the sort of high-heeled shoes that are supposed to go with attainment, on their way to another day with the computer, or the Stock Exchange prices, or an important presentation, or a client to be exhaustively entertained. And after a day of this they get to meet their friends in a wine bar, where, over a bottle of Frascati, they decide where to go for the evening. Their talk resembles the after-hours conversation of men. 'What a day I've had!' they cry to each other. 'I'm exhausted! You have no idea how the market is behaving at the moment. I've had New York on the line all day.' Bravely they will decide to eat out, although waiters still dislike women diners on their own: they are thought to be a dubious advertisement, spreading the contagion of bad luck around them, not qualifying for the full treatment. Waiters also dislike the plastic swathe of dry cleaning left in the cloakroom, but this has had to be picked up in the lunch hour, otherwise there can be no power dressing for the following day.

No, for such women I would decree a dear little

house, in some established suburb, and a leisurely walk to the shops with a basket over one arm, and an afternoon with one's feet up on the sofa, reading a magazine. The evenings of such women are a bit vague in my mind: I always assume them to be married, or possibly of independent means. Such women never venture out at night unless suitably accompanied, and of course they are always delivered safely to their door afterwards, their escort checking, at their request, the window locks and the burglar alarm. I actually know a woman who lives like this. What is extraordinary is that she is the same age as I am, and yet she lives in this time warp, as if she had no idea that this kind of existence is reserved for a dying breed, for women in their late middle or old age who perhaps worked for one or two years in their youth and then thankfully gave it up.

The lives of idle women fascinate me, and yet such women always bridle when you speak to them of your commitments, your plans, your calculations, as if you were casting aspersions on their own industriousness, which they will then go on to demonstrate. And it is true that my kind of woman rarely has time for the fine cooking, the planned shopping, or even such things as an afternoon tidying the plants in the garden. It will be a pity if women in the more conventional mould are to be phased out, for there will never be anyone to go home to. Of course, my own existence has never remotely resembled any of this, and yet I like to think about it. It pleases me, in some obscure way, to conceive of women as timorous, delicate, in need of special treatment, of deference, waves of sympathy and praise lapping at their feet as they perform some quite ordinary task, or simply preside at their tables, family acquiescent around them. Born to serve, as it might be thought, such women seem to triumph, and many of them preserve a good conscience at the same time. It is quite an achievement. It was for the pleasure of watching this phe-

171

nomenon at its best that I was initially fascinated by the Livingstones. Beautifully at ease with her conscience, Dorrie was like the virtuous woman in the Bible, anxious to see others happy, and all prospering around her. The thought of Dorrie intruding into this pleasant fantasy should have warned me that I was trying to keep unwelcome thoughts at bay, that all this vague thinking was obscuring a task which I had banished to the back of my mind, where it waited, seeking its time, always inconvenient, and destined to disrupt my own activities. But really, I thought, as December slid into January, something must have been decided by now, some agreement have been reached between Heather and her parents. I found myself reacting with increasing violence against the softness of heart that had overtaken me in those days at the hospital, against all my talk of duties and loyalties, for which, when removed from the Livingstone cause, I cared nothing. I still felt a pang of regret when I thought of the trouble that Heather's absurd decision must have stirred up by now, but for Heather herself, I felt, I regret to say, a certain contempt. To embrace so obscure a destiny was, to my mind, a feeble excuse for not doing anything else. It signified an abdication of a different sort, not the abandonment of a difficult situation, but the abandonment of a self that might have matured into just the sort of independence that the self-reliant woman must attain. After all, we are all committed to this now. That Heather should merely exchange one set of parents for a parent of a different sort seemed to me ludicrous, a desecration of all that she was leaving behind, as well as illustrating a docility that no longer had anything attractive about it. My aversion to her line of conduct was compounded by a kind of anger at the position I had adopted, almost by default, as if it should not have fallen to my lot to speak up for parents, for families, and, even more, for what I had called the life of reason,

172

as if all these things had anything to do with me, represented my true wishes, or even my true destiny. I had adopted a position which might even be false, and I had felt myself called upon to convert others to it. The discomfort involved in this process will be recognized by anyone who acts in bad faith. That was why I had visions of the sign saying CLOSED on the door.

And yet, although the outcome had proved to be so uncomfortable, I still did not see what else I could have done. It was just that I had decided not to do any more of it. If my remonstrations had had no effect, then that was unfortunate, but I was under no further obligation in the matter of Heather's behaviour. The trouble was, I reflected, that they were all so romantic. I remembered Oscar and Dorrie at the opera, hands clasped, attention sharpening, as the heroine came forward on the stage to sing of her undying and usually fatal love. I had a suspicion that if Heather told them of her feelings for this Marco they might be willing to see the elements of a great love in what was probably merely an error of judgement. For romantic love usually is fatal, and not for the reasons given by the heroine on stage. And if one embarks on it one must be prepared for a state which is very nearly all loss. Romantic love is either for the very gullible or the very brave, and I had no conviction that Heather was very brave, although I had no doubt that she was gullible, probably in the wrong sense. This adventure of hers could lead to permanent exile, for which she was lamentably unprepared. She, who had been cared for all her life, would be vanishing into the unknown and would be without occupation, stranded in a web of circumstances which she had no means of understanding. And in her memory she would un- doubtedly revert with nostalgia and with regret to the life she had left behind her, the life of just such a woman as I had been thinking about, correct and tranquil and protected.

173

For she would never come home again. I saw that quite clearly. She would live down to her new situation, and her parents, bewildered, would wonder what had become of her. The essence of romantic love is that wonderful beginning, after which sadness and impossibility may become the rule. And Oscar and Dorrie, powered by their investment in that wonderful beginning, would, by that same token, be bereft of her company. There was no reason why they should have her company for life, of course; even she had seen that, and she was not a hard-hearted girl. But they were all of the same stamp; they had peaceful expectations. It was probably on account of their peaceful expectations that they could indulge their fantasies of romantic love. For them, it would essentially be a romance, a dream, something that happened to heroines, willing to renounce the world, and dying before the world could renounce them. Those who survive such an experience have been forced to learn a hard lesson, and it does not always improve them. Love, any kind of love, contains such lessons. Not all are capable of learning them.

I could hear myself sighing as I moved towards the telephone, committing myself once again to the fortunes of the Livingstones. Heather, for some reason, I dared not face. I felt that I had offended her simply by virtue of being myself, as if I had failed some vital test of worthiness by advertising my own fall from innocence. I also knew – and this could not be altered – that everyone falls from innocence sooner or later, shedding the earlier self and its illusions to assume the wary guise of a mature adult. It was by no stretch of the imagination my fault if I had already entered this state and Heather had not. Nevertheless, I felt the shame that comes with the feeling of having despoiled something, although Heather continued to irritate me and her plight to strike me as extravagant, ridiculous, and damaging.

I had also felt a measure of relief in speaking to her so

brutally, as if the time had come to shed all the euphemisms with which her life was shrouded. Although I knew the reasons for the failure of her marriage I felt that the actual divorce would be dealt with daintily and its cause never be revealed or acknowledged. Heather would then no doubt be declared in need of a holiday, and little compensations would be offered, as if she had not so much suffered (I doubt if any real suffering were involved) as been mildly insulted. Oh, I know such women, women who, like Ophelia, turn all to favour and to prettiness. These are the women who say, 'I'm afraid I was a little bit naughty', after committing some gross misdemeanour, or 'I'm afraid I got rather cross', after screaming their way to victory. Women like this have always existed: they still do, in spite of all the changes that have taken place. I simply cannot put up with them, or with their conviction that Nanny is still somewhere in the background. Better by far to be glum but truthful, piercing a few clouds of deceit, matching the word to the thought or to the intention. No blame should attach to telling the truth. But it does, it does. And in confining the intrinsically blameless Heather within the larger category of women whom I despise, for really quite other reasons, I felt that I had committed an offence which could not be overlooked by either of us. That was why I made no attempt to get in touch with her. Nor, of course, she with me.

But Dorrie was another matter. I had seen her near death, and I could not quite banish the sight from my mind. Even if she had escaped the knowledge of her near demise I had not. And although I had no doubt that the truth would always be hidden from her by that loving and anxious family, the truth was there. There was no avoiding it. In fact, in my eyes, the truth was rendered all the more terrible by the enthusiastic decision to ignore it that had no doubt been made on her

175

behalf. Even now I did not doubt that her convalescence was taking place on a wave of false assurances, in an attempt to expunge the sights that all had seen and none could live with. And Dorrie herself laughing at their efforts and their energy, protesting that this was not necessary, that she was perfectly all right, that they were making too much of a fuss. Perhaps their very commitment to the task would sow a tiny seed of doubt in her mind, and she would look across at Oscar, sitting so calmly in his usual chair, his newspaper across his lap, while her excited sisters ran to and fro with little trays of food to tempt her. And he would look up, would smooth down his tie with his fine dry hand, would say, 'All right, darling?' And for a time at least she would be all right.

Heather's part in all this I could not quite see. She would not be needed at these daily rituals, so essentially a conspiracy among adults which might risk destruction at younger hands. Heather's part in all this would be her absence, but with that absence, in which they could compound all their pretences, the knowledge, the promise, that Heather would visit them at the weekend, as she always had, as she used to in the days before her marriage, and would sit there, amiable, blank-faced, without mystery, subsumed once again into the matrix of her family, as if everything that had happened to her in the recent past had been an illusion, a myth put about to frighten them. Heather was simply required not to change. It might be difficult for her, I could see that, but why should she not encounter a little difficulty? She had the stamina for it. She would know which part was hers to play. After all, she was very shrewd. I persisted in thinking this, although, when I turned it over in my mind, I could not remember a single circumstance in which Heather had ever demonstrated her legendary shrewdness. Nevertheless, I knew it to be there.

My hesitation and my faint-heartedness were com-

176

pounded by the fact that about that time it rained heavily for a part of every day, usually in the morning, so that I awoke to streaming windows and that sense of oppression that always accompanies wet weather. This is not mere antipathy (nobody likes rain, after all) but a terrible nervousness that connects with my other fears. I cannot look at weeping skies or raindrops pattering on windows, or, least of all, at the falling rain itself without getting up to wander nervously from room to room, wringing my hands, and wondering if I can last out until it stops. And if I am out, of course, it is a hundred times worse. With every splash of water on my face or my leg I have to suppress an involuntary cry. In the end I have to run for cover, and end up buying something I never use in the nearest shop to hand. If I am at home, I try not to look at the windows, but I find I am drawn to them, as if made to watch, repelled yet fascinated by the falling sheet of water, wondering what it would be like to stand in it and let my head fall back and my mouth and eyes fill. But this, of course, is to be resisted, as is any kind of relaxation of my vigilance. The temptation is both horrifying and enduring, and can never be resolved.

My mission, however, was to enquire after Dorrie's health, and to find out what had happened to Heather and her romance. If, as I hoped, the idea had quietly subsided and she were back in the fold there would be nothing more for me to do, for I could hardly add to what I had already said, nor could I even allude to it. Perhaps we could all be as we had been before, a little circle which I was occasionally permitted to join. Perhaps we could again be that nest of gentlefolk, the idea of which had once so beguiled me. The idea, in fact, rather than the reality, for reality is neither static nor shapely: reality is for the most part inconvenient. The real part of this acquaintanceship had held up a mirror in which I saw myself: forlorn, uncherished,

177

unaccompanied. For all I knew this was the way I was seen not merely by myself but by the Livingstones as well. Various discomforts – the monotonous falling water, the vision of myself as a poor orphan, and my recent outburst, perhaps, above all, my recent outburst – kept me from enquiring after Dorrie's health until well into January.

When I finally made the call it was answered by Dorrie, who sounded delighted to hear from me.

'We wondered what had happened to you, dear. Of course we know how tired you must be after Christmas and we didn't like to bother you.'

'It's lovely to hear your voice, Dorrie. How are you?'

'Oh, I'm getting along splendidly, dear. And they're all making such a fuss of me. Anyone would think I'd been really ill.' She laughed doubtfully. 'And I'm not allowed to do a thing.'

Her voice had recovered its vigour, with perhaps a slightly breathy overtone which I put down to the temporary wound in her throat.

'Rachel?' she went on. 'We'd love to see you, dear. Are you by any chance free tomorrow afternoon? I've told the girls to go out for the day. They've been so good, here all the time. But I've put my foot down. And it would be such a lovely chance to have a really good talk with you. I know Oscar would love to see you.'

'How is he?' I asked.

'Just fine, bless him. Can we expect you tomorrow, then? The usual time. You know the way, dear.'

Although her greeting had been so warm my reluctance strangely persisted. Perhaps because by now I knew too much, because, in fact, I knew more than any of them, I felt an instinctive desire to avoid that lovely talk that Dorrie had promised me. There was too much that I would not be entitled to say. I felt poisoned by my knowledge: this was perhaps my equivalent of original sin. Although the rain had died down to a fine drizzle I stopped the first taxi I saw coming and settled down in the back for what might well be an afternoon of great difficulty, in which dissimulation must be my lot, and further discomfort its inevitable accompaniment.

The house, as I stood outside it, seemed smaller than I had remembered, and the garden less immaculate: one drowned rose hung limply from its stem. When Oscar opened the door to me, and smiled at me as he had always done, I felt reassured, but as I followed him into the drawing-room I was aware of a miasma of forgotten meals, or of the hasty housekeeping of the sisters in an alien kitchen. I was aware of the much breathed air of convalescence, the contagion of the flesh thrusting its persistent memory forward into a time in which it might be thought to be irrelevant. I found myself nervous of what I might see, but Dorrie, seated in her usual chair (but in it, not on the edge of it as hitherto) greeted me delightedly and with conviction. She looked astonishingly well. Her hair had been done in a new and flattering way to hide the mutilated earlobe, and it made her look younger. She wore a skirt and cardigan of dark blue raw silk, and into the opening of the inevitable print blouse she had tucked a silk scarf to hide the tiny wound in her throat. She looked, if anything, better than I had seen her for a long time. Her honeysuckle scent floated on the waves of warmth emanating from the radiators, which were, as always, turned up to their highest register. Bowls and vases of flowers added their exudations to the heady atmosphere.

I had always thought her a pretty woman, and here, in her natural setting, she appeared to her best advantage. There were few signs of age about her beyond a slight blurring of the outlines of face and figure. The upper part of the body was still fine, but the waist was beginning to sink into the saddle of the hips, which would eventually give her an appearance of shortness

179

and plumpness, although she was in fact very neatly made. I noticed the legs in that passive elderly position again, the ankles crossed, the knees splayed slightly outwards. But the face was still that of a good-looking youngish woman. Perhaps there was a pad of flesh under the chin, perhaps there were lines describing a parenthesis around the mouth, but the eyebrows were not yet untidy and they arched magnificently above the mild blue eyes. That expression, described so long ago, was still familiar to me. It quested, in an unhurried way, and appeared to be looking, above a crowd of heads, for a well-loved face. Where? Where? it appeared to be saying. I remembered Oscar's eternal question: 'Where's your mother?' But she was here, beside us both, looking well and happy, and there was no need to seek any further.

And yet there was one huge question in the air. Where was Heather and where would she be in the future? When would she come back to them, and how would they find her? This matter lay untouched as we exchanged our compliments and pleasantries, as the tea was made and brought in, as Oscar handed me a cup and a plate, and Dorrie protested at the smallness of my appetite. My appetite had in fact died on me as soon as I had entered the house. And it was not Dorrie, all animation and pleasure, who retained my attention: it was Oscar. Immaculate and benign as ever, there was a thoughtfulness, a scruple, a pursing of the lips, a holding apart, even as he joined in our conversation. I could see it was an effort for him to concentrate on the banalities that were being offered and which were clearly a preliminary to what was to follow, the main business of the day. I sensed more reserve in him than usual, although he had always kept his own counsel. I felt he was mounting a watch, and was, behind his placid exterior, alert for misconstructions, for evasions of the truth – for the truth must now be faced – but also for hurt and injury. It would fall to his lot to recognize the truth but also to mediate it, lest it fall too heavily on the one who had already been weakened.

What remained incredible to me was that Heather, a girl as dull as her name, should have gathered about her such an aura of fatality. But perhaps it was only I who felt this; perhaps I was beginning to find a symbolism in her undistinguished adventure and the light it was shedding on my own life. Its effect on me had already been disproportionate. After all, she was not really my concern. But she had startled me into a recognition of our differences, had made me uneasy in a way which I did not fully understand, had driven me to a pitch of opposition which had something murderous about it. And throughout all these convolutions of mood she had barely appeared, and when she had, there was not one word of her sparse discourse that could be construed as having any intention or flavour. What was happening was happening almost by inadvertence, which made it all the more frightening. It was as if Heather had already removed herself, but had in doing so affected all who knew her.

But perhaps I was the only one so affected. Her parents sat there, thoughtfully drinking tea, as if nothing could ever disrupt the tenor of lives so established, so comfortable. Outside the leaded windows of the warm and scented room a drowned world vaguely materialized, for the vapour in the atmosphere lingered and the wet pavements evaporated only slowly in the grey air. As the light of that uncertain day faded, it seemed as if it might pass altogether without a single word of any significance being exchanged. The Livingstones were discussing whether or not to go to Spain, or rather when to go: reasons for going or not going were put forward, but this seemed to me a theoretical exercise for I saw no sign in their settled carefulness that they would ever leave that room. I felt that there was

181

something ritualistic about this discussion, as if it were being aired purely *pour la forme*. I also felt that there was something collusive about it, as if my own presence, my potential contribution, were being held off. They were, without properly realizing what they were about, on the defensive. Finally, unable to tolerate the tension they had unconsciously set up, I asked, 'How is Heather?'

Dorrie cleared her throat. 'She's very well, dear. You've heard her news, I suppose?'

'Her news?'

'Yes. She's going to get married again. We're very pleased for her.'

'I see,' I said slowly. I was determined to say very little, knowing that I had already said too much.

'Yes, to Chiara's brother. It's all very romantic. Apparently it was love at first sight.' Dorrie looked at me brightly. Something of our discussion had obviously reached her.

'It won't be like last time,' she went on, with a gesture of dismissal. 'I'm afraid Michael was too young to be a proper husband. I blame myself for encouraging him. And, you know, Oscar never really took to him.'

I looked at Oscar, whose face was set in lines of melancholy dignity. It was his other expression, the one I always thought of as peculiarly his. Oh, why so sad? I had once thought. But now it was as if he had always known that he was to sustain a loss for which nothing could compensate.

'When will she leave?' I asked, watching him carefully.

'Oh, she's already gone, dear. Didn't she let you know? I expect she was in too great a hurry. She had such a lot to do before she left.'

There was a pause. 'You'll miss her,' I said.

It was Oscar who answered. He sighed. 'Yes, we'll miss her. But you see, Rachel, she must have her chance.'

'Her chance?'

'Her chance to be as happy as we have been.'

He moved across to Dorrie and took her hand. They faced me as if facing some sort of tribunal.

'She wasn't happy, Rachel,' said Dorrie. 'She said nothing to me, but I knew. And she's always been such a good girl. When she explained to us how she wanted to live, we understood. Didn't we, Oscar? We wouldn't want her to stay here just on our account. After all, we won't always be here.' She smiled sadly. 'And we'd rather know that she had had this chance. I didn't like to think of her growing older and not knowing what true love was.'

'But how do you know . . . ?' I began, in spite of myself.

'We saw her face,' Dorrie said simply. 'We knew.'

So had they known during those nights at the opera, when the heroine, transformed, came forward to sing her aria. Simple intimations, to be ignored by those of us who had seen it all before and who in any case knew the ending, but incontrovertible proof for those of a more trusting disposition. I looked at them in despair. They were both sad now, but noble and resigned, as if the emotions of the theatre had invaded their ordinary, their so ordinary lives. It was what I had been summoned to hear, of course. And yet it did not convince me. This romanticism of theirs was a little too prepared, too official, as if assumed for the occasion. They were not subtle people and I did not doubt for a moment that they believed what they had said. But nothing had broken through their rationalizations, nothing to persuade me that Heather's decision had been completely internalized. They had accepted it, but more had happened than they would ever let me know. In fact I sensed that they wanted to deflect any comments or questions that I might care to put. I think they were afraid of what I might say.

'Well, I must be getting back.' I busied myself as one does to announce imminent departure. 'You'll let me know how to get in touch with her when you have an address.' An absurd remark, I reflected: they must already have an address. But I did not want to give the impression that I was intruding, or had any intention of intruding, into what was clearly a family affair.

'Of course, dear. Oscar, wrap that fruit cake in foil for Rachel to take home.'

When he was out of the room, she leaned forward and whispered, 'He's a little upset, it's only natural. But he'll get over it. We're both of one mind.' She was looking paler, and lines of tiredness had appeared in her face. 'Oscar,' she said, as he reappeared, a greaseproof paper parcel in one hand. 'Tell Rachel she's to go on just as before. To come and see us just as she always used to.' She gripped my arm painfully. 'We shall rely on you, you know. I dare say we shall miss her.' She burst into tears, searching blindly for a handkerchief and turning her face away.

Oscar's arms were round her. 'All right, darling, all right. She's over-tired,' he said to me.

'Yes, of course,' I replied. 'I'll leave you now. I'll telephone tomorrow. Don't cry, Dorrie,' I said, kneeling in front of her. 'It will be all right.'

Her hand reached out and stroked my face. 'If only I could see her again,' she whispered. 'If only she were here.'

With strange stiff movements I got to my feet. I knew now why I had come, what everything that had gone before had been leading up to. Oh, why so sad? For there was never any doubt that I would play my subordinate part to the end. I would not come here again, that was clear. The divisions between us were too real to be glossed over. But there was one more thing I had to do.

'If you like,' I said, 'I will go and see her. Bring her

back for a visit. Would you like that?'

Dorrie's drowned face looked up at me. 'Would you?' she said, still whispering. 'Would you go there?'

'Why not?' I replied cheerfully. 'I was going to Italy anyway. We're very quiet in the shop at this time of year. I usually take my holiday about now. I'll go and have a look round, if you like. Get a clearer picture. And then she can come home with me. She'll probably be glad of the break.'

I left quickly after that, wishing to spare myself the exclamations of gratitude that I knew would come my way. I remember Dorrie's sudden pacification, the restoration of a little colour to her face, the falling back in the chair as if exhausted. When she kissed me, her wet cheek lay on mine for a long time. I remember Oscar standing at the door of the house to wave me goodbye: I was aware of him standing there, but I only turned once to raise my hand in farewell. I drifted through the chill streets as if dreaming, barely noticing the dark and the loneliness. It had been a disrupted day, a day when I had broken with my Spartan working habits, only to be immersed in the troubled waters of a family drama. I ached with longing for the structure of a normal day, with all the intrigues and adventures confined within the covers of books, and all the books arranged alphabetically by author. Yet I felt no compulsion to get back to the shop. The effect of the afternoon had been to cut me off from reality, so that it seemed to me as if the rest of my life lay before me quite empty, quite aimless, and my only task or mission was to retrieve Heather from her hiding place and bring her safely home again.

My anger was slow to gather but when it came at last it was monumental. It was also quite cold. I coldly reviewed the plans I would have to make, and prepared for my absence as if I might never return. By the end of the following day all my travel arrangements had been made: tickets booked, letters written, bills paid, Robin

185

alerted. The fact that I had no notion of where Heather was to be found did not seem to hinder me. On the off chance I sent a telegram to the Gritti Palace, remembering that she had once said that she called in there every day. I had no doubt that I would find her, probably in a passive position, in a public place, waiting to be led back. I had visions of myself arresting her outside Quadri's. And if she did not want to follow me? She was hardly under compulsion, and there was the shadowy figure of Marco in the background to be reckoned with. But I was by now so angry that I saw myself sweeping him aside, taking her by the wrist, throwing her on to the plane, delivering her into the arms of her father, and stalking off, never to speak to any of them again.

My anger was of course mixed with fear. I knew Venice but always avoided it. It was the ultimate nightmare: a city filled with water. It was bad enough in the summer, when it was neutralized by crowds of visitors: one could always join a group when crossing a bridge and thus not lose touch with corporeality. But in late winter, deserted, misty, half sunk, it would unnerve me. My own trepidation would be a factor in the forthcoming exchange. I too might fail through inadvertence.

It was the anger that saved me. I nurtured it as if it were a sacred flame, a talisman that would protect me throughout this journey into the unknown. Without it I would have felt enormously at risk; with it I felt cold, hard, a bully, a brute. With it I could commit murder. And while my victim, in all innocence, sat at a table in some dingy apartment, waiting for her prospective mother-in-law to serve her with a plate of soup, I armed myself with courage, sought out my finest clothes, smoothed the leather of conqueror's boots against the calves of my legs, slammed the door on my flat, as if the place were of no consequence to me, and walked out

186

into the street, the dearest place on earth to me at that moment, my face haughty with disapproval.

I did not telephone the Livingstones before I left. My feelings were too mixed to enable me to give them my full attention. Waves of panic and fury threatened my equilibrium: I was not in the mood to offer palliatives. I should have warned them that I was not the best person for this mission, that an aunt, safely backed up by an uncle, a cousin, should have gone in my place, but I remembered them at the hospital, all bereft, devoid of initiative, weakened by tears, and I dismissed the thought. In some curious way – and this was what kept my anger at full strength – I was being used as the most competent member of their entourage to perform this impossible task. I was being seen as tough, and it was true that I gave that impression. No protection was to be afforded me: that was the message. I was in this world to fend for myself, eternally. When I thought of this, Heather's plight became quite irrelevant. She was merely the pretext for a display of strength that would be forced from me, as if I must live out the fiction that they all entertained. As I got into the first taxi that came along – and it came along very quickly, much too quickly – I vowed silently that if Heather were to make me suffer one moment longer than was necessary I would have a reckoning with her that she would never forget.

E L E V E N

I MET an amusing man on the plane, with whom I exchanged addresses. We agreed that he should telephone me in a couple of days' time, when we would meet and have dinner. The flight was uneventful. I bought myself a large bottle of scent from the stewardess and tried to believe that I was going on holiday.

I had booked a room at the Pensione Wildner, hoping that it would overlook the back, but here luck was against me, and I had an uninterrupted view of the Grand Canal. I was shaken on arrival, as I knew I should be, by the ride in the water taxi from the airport. Shooting between the posts that marked the passage for traffic in the uneven rocking expanse, or bucketing in the wake of a larger craft, the tiny launch seemed to expend enormous effort just to skim the surface. As I cowered in the little cabin, wincing every time we struck a wave, I could feel the beat of my heart in my throat, in my stomach, and willed myself to a scrupulous calm. It was raining, of course: through the spattered windows I could make out only a swelling sea of grey. Sky and water seemed to merge in a dull uniformity. Low cloud and watery swell, combined with the jittery motion of the launch, made me fear for my powers of endurance, which, I think, up to that point, had never let me down. Venice, a rim, a crust of buildings, barely visible above the horizon, looked as if it were buried in the sea. I marvelled at the insouciance of Venetians, forever stepping on and off boats, bridging that uneasy gap of water with a negligent foot, ignoring the cats that slipped along like shadows, worshipping in bravura churches poised on promontories or islands. A mineral city, sprouting well-heads instead of trees and bridges instead of gardens. And devoid of that expansive, almost operatic, and always endearing good humour that characterizes the centre of Italy or even its farther coast. Venetians were doleful, subtle people, not given to loud voices, public eating and drinking, or effusive gestures of greeting or affection. Even the children were quiet. This I remembered from my previous stay, which had been in the early days of a beautiful summer. I had on that occasion been subdued in mood, an effect of the silence and the immobility of the city. Gondolas, gliding in the dark green caverns of canals, had seemed propelled by the agency of a dream. But now the city looked devoid even of that silent life. It rode low in the water, unconvincing. I wondered how it could sustain the weight of stone it had imposed on itself. It is apparently sinking. But it must always have appeared to be sinking, and perhaps the world is willing to believe that it might be, so vainglorious, so utterly irrational and challenging is its disposition. Its ultimate demise will be accepted as a punishment for spiritual pride.

Yet, as always, once out of the wretched little boat, and relatively safe on relatively dry land, I found it curiously humdrum. Stout black-clad figures with oil-cloth bags slipped into dark shops pungent with sweating sausage, or lingered by windows occupied by tall glass jars in which floated olives or small blanched cheeses. In the Piazza San Marco, which was always smaller than I thought it would be, there was already a party of schoolchildren, meek faces under gondoliers' straw hats, eyes turning towards the pigeons, away from the church whose mosaics they had been sent to study. Weak and desultory Viennese melodies were being sawn on inexpert violins as I took my first cup of coffee there. The city was quiet, for few visitors would choose to come so early in the season, when the mists made the air clammy and frequent rainstorms pocked

189

the surface of the water. Even as I sat I saw the sky darken, and a brief bolt of lightning ushered in a flood of silver rain: some hidden light in the atmosphere illuminated the heavy drops as they struck the ground and bounced up again, translucent as fishes. A bell boomed the hour. With a sigh I picked up my bag and paid my bill. Then I set out to look for Heather.

In my telegram I had told her where I would be staying, and I assumed that she would leave a message there. But some instinct had urged me to drop my bag in my room and to hasten away without asking for my letters. I had this absurd idea, which was nevertheless extremely tenacious, that I would find her in the street somewhere. In my mind I could see her quite clearly, motionless, in her black garments, poised to vanish into some dark alley. But I would be there before her, spirited and relentless in my fine leather boots, and I would take her by the arm and lead her back in triumph to the Pensione Wildner, where I would sit her on the bed and invite her to a final accounting.

I set off, therefore, without aim or direction, striking inland wherever I could. Of course the water eternally intruded, but I marked off for future reference a tiny bar on a corner, with two small metal tables outside. Janus-like, it faced two ways. If I took up my stance at one of the tables, I could command a wide sweep of the little square, which had the advantage of many entrances and exits, rather like a stage set. A broad-hipped church stood modestly off-centre. A child, muffled in scarves, one of which was crossed over its chest and tied behind its back, chased a ball round my feet. 'Marco, Marco,' called its mother. This seemed like a sign. I ordered another cup of coffee and increased my vigilance.

Apart from looking for Heather there was nothing that I wanted to do. I had not chosen to come here, after all, nor would I ever voluntarily choose so watery a place for my delectation. As the grey day wore on I found myself at a loss. Frequent showers of rain kept me dodging from café to café, staring out from behind silver-streaming windows for a glimpse of that black-clad figure. Time seemed to be passing very slowly. I had lunch, then forced myself to go to the Accademia. The gold polyptychs of what seemed to me a primeval time gleamed dully in the high wooden arched rooms; short flights of stairs floated me down to more altar-pieces, curious repositories of mournfulness on these secular walls. The flailing limbs of several martyrdoms assailed me. There seemed to be no visitors. I sought the refuge of corridors, unable to tolerate those dark floating spaces. Bellini's Madonnas turned cheeks shadowed with sorrow in my direction, their heads describing an arc of grief which nevertheless excluded my inheritance. In a deserted room I found the only picture I wanted to see. The woman suckling her child had a heavy face, immanent with meaning, but from which all explanation had been withdrawn. To her right, on the left of the picture, stood the mysterious and elegant knight, intense and remote, his face in shadow. The storm that broke on the scene bound the two together in puzzling complicity. In the background, a banal hill village. In the middle distance, two broken columns.

I took a walk that kept me looking alertly round corners, gazing into the faces that I willed to meet mine. I was getting used to the place now, no longer searched hesitantly with my foot to see if the land were still dry, turned up my coat collar against the rain, thought of telephoning the man I had met on the plane. I tried to withdraw my attention from the task in hand, and even managed to do so for a little while, until it reclaimed me with the fading of the light. As darkness began to fall I hesitantly retraced my steps to the Pensione Wildner, and reluctantly took up residence in the room overlooking the Grand Canal. From my window I could see the

191

big boats riding at anchor. I could pick out their names, painted in white on the sheer black sides: Maximus, Validus, Strenuus, Ausus, Ludus. With a sigh I turned to the bed and unpacked my bag. The melancholy of the traveller whom nobody has been designated to meet filled the silent space around me. It was with a great effort that I took off my raincoat, the uniform without which I was no longer on guard, and my boots, chosen instruments with which I would quarter Venice until I found my prey, and ran a bath. There was a restaurant down below, and if I did not mind the darkened lapping water that was my horizon I would dine there and retire early, in preparation for another day. The following day, I was sure, would bring me victory. And I thought in terms of victory and defeat, for now I knew that I was engaged in some sort of contest, in which either Heather or I would triumph and with us the vindication of our claims. It seemed to me at that moment that our entire lives were on trial, and it was a matter of some anxiety to me that I should not fail this test, that my hardworking and eminently reasonable existence should be given full marks. I felt as if this whole adventure were a tournament, at which unseen onlookers waited to be persuaded of my ultimate validity. I am not normally given to such romancing, yet the combination of the dark night, the empty room, the too lavish meal that I had ordered and which I was suddenly too tired to eat, made me fearful, like a subject nation, waiting to be overcome by a stronger power. I tried to assume a nonchalance which I did not feel and turned my head deliberately to the canal. A water bus ploughed indifferently along at high speed. It suddenly occurred to me that I might have to travel along hidden ways to find Heather, and I saw myself forced to venture out into the open sea. Yet she would not unnecessarily torment me; I knew that. She was too calm, too fair, too indifferent. And her indifference to my fate would secure her the victory if I were not extremely on my guard. That was why I must prepare for the following day with due care.

I slept heavily, although I woke once or twice to the spectacle of passing lights dimly reflected on the ceiling of my room. When I awoke finally, some time after eight o'clock, I saw that it had rained heavily in the night but was now fine, with a pearl grey light that seemed to have trapped some vestige of a remote sun. When I had dressed, I went downstairs with a heart which was, in spite of myself, somewhat lighter. I noticed a letter in the pigeon-hole to which a silent porter returned my key. I took it out to breakfast with me, deliberately keeping it by my plate, unopened, until I had drunk my coffee. Finally, when I thought I had imposed enough discipline on myself, I slit the envelope. The single sheet of paper, without salutation, read: 'I will meet you outside the Gritti at twelve noon today, Wednesday.' It was signed, simply, 'Heather'.

Suddenly I felt genial, good-natured. It was as if in replying to my summons Heather had placed herself in my hands. Our forthcoming meeting seemed to me no less crucial than hitherto, but I no longer felt strongly about the outcome. I relinquished the idea of hand-cuffing her and removing her by force; in fact in a curious way I was willing to concede that she might do as she pleased. Merely by confronting her I would have acted as a reminder. There was no longer any point in telling her to be sensible. But by simply standing before her, meeting her on her own ground, forcing her out into the open, I would provide a pointed comment on her secrecy, her concealment. I would demystify her, tear down the edifice of this great love which could not stand the light of day but must burrow down through the back streets of Venice, clothed in uniform black. Like the child in the story, I would point to the emperor's non-existent new clothes and ask politely in what ways they differed from the old ones. Then she

193

would have to attempt, stumblingly, if I knew her, to justify her conduct. I did not demand that she renounce her Marco and follow me home: in my new mood of realism I saw that that would be unlikely. I would simply ask her why she had, apparently with a perfectly good conscience, caused such an upheaval. I would ask if this amorous commotion were really appropriate and whether it would not have been kinder to manage it some other way, whether forsaking all others were to be taken so literally that I should have to endure this pilgrimage simply for the chance of being granted an interview.

My time was my own until twelve o'clock, but I found myself hard put to fill it with incident. It had resolved itself into pure waiting, and with the recognition of this state came dangerous intimations, driftings and longings that I had thought I had entirely forsaken. I settled down to a morning of coffee drinking, desultory exploring, examining of faces. I knew the route I had to take: across the Piazza, past San Moisè, across a tiny bridge to the pretty eventless square in which I had watched the child with the ball the previous day. After a fruitless hour in which I selected and then disheartened-ly rejected churches that might be visited, I made my way back to the little Bar Ducale where I decided to sit out the intervening time. I had nothing to read. Indeed, I had come prepared only to look for Heather, not to divert myself. I sat in a trance-like state, trying to will back into myself something of that tonic anger with which I had set out on this quest. But there seemed to be no anger to hand today. My earlier good humour had entirely disappeared, and with it the rigid armature that normally sustained my days. I was at a loss. My amusements were too secret, too deliberate to spread themselves into the benign air of the working week, and now even that week had been taken away from me. A pale sun came out; water glinted shiftily behind me. As the half hour boomed mutedly from a distant campanile I started up in fright, thinking that I must have missed something, a clue, a means of cutting short this abominable visit. For if the anger had left me, the fear seemed to be returning. '*Ancora*,' I said to the waiter, indicating my cup. For suddenly there was nothing for me to do but sit there until the chimes of another bell were to release me.

At half past eleven I got up. I had forgotten whether she had asked me to meet her inside or outside the Gritti, and, if inside, whether in the bar or in one of the salons. And if in one of the salons, which one? I strolled as carelessly as I could into the lobby. On the terrace, perhaps? That was the obvious and most pleasant place for a talk. But she had not mentioned the terrace, I remembered: I would have retained the sound of the word if she had. If she were staying there I might enquire for the number of her room, but I had this tenacious feeling that she was somewhere else, her tracks covered, at an address that her father, having heard it only on the telephone, confessed that he might have got wrong. In any event her address would be of no use to me. I had no intention of searching for her; the topography of Venice had always eluded me. That people might actually live there always struck me as impossible. I think I really believed that they all shipped themselves back to the mainland at nightfall and there lived entirely unremarkable lives just like everybody else, parking the car, watching television, and shopping in supermarkets. The silence of the hotel seemed to bear out my assumption that she was not there. I took a last look down a vista of deserted salons, and then resigned myself to waiting outside. As I turned to go, the concierge closed his great book with an air of finality, as if ringing down the curtain on the day. It was quite clear that he would allow nothing untoward to happen within the walls of his precinct, that he would stand stalwart behind his desk to repel intruders. Our conversation therefore must take place on neutral ground.

I wandered up and down outside, turned the corner, and then I saw her. Or rather them, for she was accompanied by a man whom I took to be Marco. She was, as I had expected, dressed in black, and so was he, a tall slim black-haired man in black trousers and a black blouson jacket, a black scarf round his neck. Heather herself was wrapped in a black shawl-like garment, through the sleeves of which, obviously obeying some injunction of his, she suddenly thrust her arms. From the slight distance at which I observed them they looked exactly alike. I remembered with a jolt how closely she had resembled Michael at her wedding, and I just had time to wonder whether this twin-like capacity of hers might not play her false in exactly the same way as it had before. But the two of them, engaged in conversation, did not have the factitious appearance that had so worried me the first time that I thought about it. What they were saying appeared to be entirely serious. They stood face to face in the middle of the square, not looking about them, not anxious, not reluctant, not fearful. I wondered how much Italian she knew or whether he spoke English. In any event, she looked completely at home. She lifted a hand to his arm and he strode off, disappearing down one of the dark exits, between a pharmacy and a blank-faced building that gave nothing away.

Heather came towards me, expressing no surprise at my presence. 'Hello,' she said. 'How are you? Shall we sit down somewhere?' And without breaking her stride she held out her hand to usher me along the same path as herself and guided me to the same little bar at which I had spent most of the morning. Seated, I felt as if I were a guest in her house. She ordered two coffees and then lit a cigarette, something I had never seen her do before. 'I didn't know you smoked,' I said stupidly. 'Oh, now

and then,' she said. 'You don't, do you?' And she put
away the packet, shook an amber bracelet further up her
wrist, and drank her coffee.

Since she had apparently nothing to say, and since I
was certainly not going to launch an appeal, I addressed
myself to my cup and covertly studied her appearance.
She had never previously struck me as attractive, having
too mulish an air, which seemed to imply a passive,
even a dormant nature. Only the long jet earrings that I
knew so well seemed to have been added to give the face
some sense of decoration. Her fine skin was innocent of
colour, as were her pale lips. Only the dark eyes, under
the arching black brows, betrayed some sign that
unknown factors, to which I had no access, had entered
her life. She gazed past me, looking preoccupied and
faintly melancholy, rather as her father might have
done. Finally, as if having reached some resolution, she
turned to me, smiled, and said, 'I suppose you've come
to tell me to go home.'

'I think you might give it some thought, yes,' I said.

'Oh, I have, I have.'

'And what have you decided?'

She laughed. 'It was all decided long ago. Didn't they
tell you? I'm afraid you've had a wasted journey,
Rachel. Unless you're on holiday, of course.'

'I came because your mother wanted to know how
you are. How you are living. She is pining, I think.'

'I'll go home soon and see them. In the meantime you
can tell her that I'm perfectly happy. I'm living here,
with Marco and his mother, and I propose to go on
doing so.'

I stared at her. She was quite composed, quite normal. She had gained something, authority, perhaps, but
it was, as ever, understated. I saw then that I had no
hope of getting her to change her mind. I tried once
more.

'What about all that you've left behind you? Your

own home. Your parents. The shop. Your own *life*, Heather.'

'My life is here,' she said.

'But you could have had it all. You could have had Marco, too. People manage. Why go to such extremes? It may seem all right now, but in ten years' time? Supposing you change your mind?'

'Oh, I don't think I will.'

'And what am I to tell them? That you've gone for ever? That they'll never see you again?'

'There's no need to tell them anything. They understand.'

'I'm sorry, Heather. I don't see it. I came here to talk sense and you don't want to listen. I suppose I've failed.'

'Oh, no,' she said. 'You've succeeded beyond all expectations.'

'Succeeded? Then . . . '

'Not this time, Rachel. The last time. When we spoke in my flat. The day Mummy was so ill.'

'I don't understand you,' I said impatiently. 'What do you mean?'

'When you told me about that other life you wanted me to lead. Deceit. Control. Arrangements. Mismanagement.'

'*Mismanagement?*' I nearly shouted, stung to fury. 'You call my life mismanagement? But you're living a fantasy, Heather. Oh, I've said all this before. I'm not going to go through it all again. But I'm sorry I've given you the impression that my life is *mismanaged*.' I was breathing hard. 'I do the best I can,' I said, more quietly. 'And if I should have liked a softer option, well, nobody hears me moaning about it.'

'I think you're very brave,' she said.

'Yes.' I looked at her. 'Yes, I am brave. I've learned to be. I've learned a lot of lessons. Unlike you, I'm afraid. I've learned to keep my life to myself, not to belabour others with it. I've learned not to back myself against

198

the world, because I know the world will win. Always. I've learned caution, politeness, what you call deceit, but what I call good manners. I've learned how to be alone and to put a good face on it. And you call that *mismanagement.*'

'I'm sorry if I've offended you,' she said. 'I didn't mean to. Shall we have some lunch? I'm afraid I'm busy this afternoon.'

'Have lunch by all means,' I told her. 'I couldn't eat a thing.'

'Then I think I'd better go. The only thing is, I had one or two things for Mummy and I wanted you to take them home. I left them in the flat. Could you meet me later, for a minute or two? Here? About five? I won't keep you. Just a couple of little things to cheer her up. I know what she likes.'

She stood up to go. I made no effort to detain her. I felt too bitter and too disgusted. My rage had subsided, leaving me feeling chilled in the misty air. The coffee I had drunk had made me nervous and my hands trembled slightly. I flung down a handful of coins and turned up the collar of my eternal raincoat. The afternoon stretched emptily before me. One thing I could do, I thought: I could book my ticket home for the following day. I would never come back to this place again. Failure was in my mouth like ashes.

I strode off in the direction of the Piazza San Marco. Pigeons infested the sky, which was clouding over. I pushed my way past the lunchtime crowds and made straight for the Pensione. It seemed to me imperative to retrieve something from this day, which was turning out so badly. I sat on my bed in my raincoat, wondering what to do next. What surprised me was the hatred that seemed to have sprung up between us. I had always thought her a dull person, hardly a woman at all, and she had apparently thought of me in the same way. Or perhaps she had simply thought me irrelevant, marginal. The curse of happy families again, so absorbed in themselves that they hardly perceive the reality of anyone else. I got up and paced about the room, which was dull and cold, reflecting the metallic light of the canal. I did not like myself for what I was feeling. I have never been comfortable with hatred, never found it invigorating or compensatory. Hatred seemed to me pure loss, if only for the amount of energy it absorbed. In fact, with this journey, I seemed to have entered a zone of loss, and I could not honestly see that Heather would gain from it. We had each of us inflicted wounds on the other, from which we would continue to suffer. And I had never wanted to serve as a warning to anyone. Nor, I am sure, had she. She liked to think of her life as a secret, banishing all witnesses from the scene. And I had been such a witness. She would never again feel uninspected. Even if her life turned out to be happy, she would know that there had been some dereliction, some loss of faith, even some loss of nerve. She would have left unhappiness behind her, and the discomfort of such a predicament would grow in her mind, eventually to rise up and overwhelm her.

And yet in a way I could not fault her, that was the worst of it. To strike out and claim one's own life, to impose it on others, even to embrace a caprice, was, though monstrous, sometimes admirable. Sometimes it just had to be done. And her actions would be seen by the world as acceptable, I had no doubt of that. She would, once again, have the status of a married woman, a condition which a person as conventional as herself would consider indispensable. She might even have the great love she claimed as hers. Eventually she would have children, would bring them home for a visit, and be acclaimed, simply for the fact of having passed the essential test. For that is the test, make no mistake about it. And I? I would plough on to a game middle age, and it was I who would be the audience, the reflector, the confidante, the baby-sitter. No one would know the inner workings of my life, nor would anyone enquire, thinking me to be a creature without mystery. It was I who would become untidy round the hips, and tired, more and more tired. I suppose I would still continue to visit the Livingstones and assist in a subordinate capacity at their gatherings. I would become 'poor Rachel'. Perhaps I already was.

I think that afternoon was one of the worst I have ever spent. Much later, when I looked back, I experienced discomfort, uneasiness, even grief, whenever I thought about it. Still in my raincoat, I paced the room, and when the room became intolerable to me I went out and tried to work off my tension in the misty streets, which always impeded me by turning into water. There was nothing I wanted to do except go home, bury myself in work, and try to rid myself of this curious feeling of shame which seemed to have come upon me. For the moment I was without resource. I was even without resource in my wanderings, for I shortly found myself pacing the short trajectory that would take me back to the Bar Ducale. I sat there, unmoving, for an hour, and then, as various bells for five o'clock boomed out, I saw Heather coming towards me. She appeared calm but preoccupied, as if she had passed an afternoon of indecision. She was carrying two plastic bags which she put on the table between us.

The light in the little square was fading fast, and her face seemed to me to have the same moody distant expression as the woman suckling her baby in the picture I had seen the previous day. Already my humble tourist excursion had vanished into the remote past. The weather, blurred and darkening, was nullifying my every activity, as if my place were simply here, and my function simply to wait. I was almost bereft of words by this time and looked to Heather for my cue.

'Well,' she said. 'Are you having a good stay? Venice

201

never disappoints, does it? Although you're not seeing it at its best.'

'There's no need for any of that, Heather. I didn't come all this way to bandy pleasantries.'

'I'm not at all sure why you did come,' she said, wrinkling her brow.

'Oh, I think you are. But you're doing your best to ignore it.'

'Well, then,' she said brightly. 'When are you leaving?'

'Oh, soon, soon. Don't worry. I won't bother you again.'

'I would have asked you back to the flat, but it's a bit awkward. I think Marco would have found it a little . . . well, you know.'

'No, I don't, as a matter of fact.'

'Well, he wasn't too keen on my meeting you.'

'Couldn't you just have said I was a friend from England?'

'A friend from England?' She looked doubtful. 'I suppose I could. But, well, I tell him everything, you see. He knows about you and why you came here.'

'I'm amazed he let you out, in that case.'

She seemed quite at ease, although friendship lay in ruins between us. I felt slightly unwell. The thought of the journey ahead of me, of the ride in the water taxi, was already in my mind. For a moment the abyss of physical illness opened up in front of me until I resolutely thought it out of the way. It was nearly dark, the early dark of winter. People began to cross the square. It was clearly time to go home.

'Well, if you wouldn't mind just taking these bags to Mummy. I should be awfully grateful.'

'By all means,' I said.

'I wouldn't have asked you, but I know you'd do anything for our family. I've always thought it the nicest thing about you.'

'How dare you,' I said quietly.

Leaving the bags on the table, she got up to leave. 'Goodbye, Rachel. I'm sorry you've had such a wasted journey.' And she was gone. She seemed to vanish into the impenetrable shadows as if she had never been.

'Heather,' I shouted. 'Come back!'

I got clumsily to my feet, impeded by what seemed to me to be increasing bulk or weight. I tried to follow her, but I had only vaguely noted the direction in which she had disappeared. I ran blindly down a side street. It was intensely quiet and very dark. I stumbled against bags of rubbish stacked against walls. Then I was blocked by water. Panicking, I retraced my steps. I was in the centre of Venice, somewhere behind the Fenice, but there was no one about. I crossed a little bridge, and then another. Everything was silent. I retraced my steps once again and passed fearfully through the dusky alleys like an unquiet spirit, careful to make no sound. On the left, in the little Calle de la Vida, I saw shapes, washing hanging from lines threaded along the sides of the buildings. Crumbling stone revealed crumbling brick. I felt my way along it and was again blocked by water. I retraced my steps, anguished and disgusted by this element which slyly kept me at arm's length. As I looked back I saw a black form disappearing into a doorway.

After an age I reached the Pensione and ran a bath. I felt as if I had traversed miles of hostile territory, and I noticed in myself that peculiar deadness that comes with a recognition of defeat. I had failed, but that was not what counted. What counted was that I was guilty of an error. It was not Heather who was endangered, but myself. I felt shame, penury, and the shock of truth. Something terrible had happened. I did not see how I could ever face those who knew me. I stared around the room. Through the window I could see the big boats rocking at anchor. Their names mocked me: Maximus,

Validus, Strenuus, Ausus, Ludus. The fact of the matter was that the wonders of this earth suddenly meant nothing to me. Without a face opposite mine the world was empty; without another voice it was silent. I foresaw a future in which I would always eat too early, the first guest in empty restaurants, after which I would go to bed too early and get up too early, anxious to begin another day in order that it might soon be ended. I lacked the patience or the confidence to invent a life for myself, and would always be dependent on the lives of others.

I thought of Heather, the last time I had seen her, in her long black garments, disappearing round a corner, turning once to face me, her expression in the bad light blank but oddly significant. She had seemed to me to be at home in this disconcerting city, she who had never left her parents. She had, in some remote way, discovered a secret. She had looked at me strangely, in a way I could not immediately identify. In the middle of that night, when I awoke suddenly from a dream of drowning, I realized that her look was one of pity. Heather had realized the weight of her knowledge; she had seen too how far behind she had left us all, how far, in particular, she had left me. I last saw her vanishing down the Calle de la Vida; at least I think it was her, but I cannot be sure. All I caught sight of was a long black skirt, the glint of an earring, before she disappeared into a doorway. I never saw her again.

I believe she did go home for a visit. I learned this much later, after Dorrie's death. Months passed and I did not get in touch. It was only when I saw Oscar in the street, at the end of another summer, that I learned all this. Heather had come and gone, then returned briefly for the funeral. Then she had disappeared again. Oscar seemed unsurprised by this, as if nothing more could touch him. He was an old man now, or looked it, his former immaculate self quite gone. He smoothed down his tie in that gesture that I remembered so well, but his hand was shaky, his nails unmanicured. He told me that he had sold the house and was going to live abroad. I noticed a filmy look, as of cataracts forming, in his eyes. I promised to write, knowing that there was nothing I had to say. My last sight of him was of an untidy figure stumping off in the direction of Marble Arch. I saw his back, bent, silhouetted against the glow of a rapidly sinking sun.

Anita Brookner is the author of the best-selling
Hotel du Lac as well as the novels *A Start in Life, Providence,*
Look at Me, and *Family and Friends.*
An international authority on eighteenth-century painting,
Brookner teaches at the Courtauld Institute
of Art and has also written *Watteau,*
The Genius of the Future, Grueze,
and *Jacques-Louis David.*